THE SECRET MOUNTAIN

"I feel… I feel…" Laura murmured distantly.

"What?" asked Peggy, without looking up from her diary.

"I feel… I want to go on," said Laura emphatically. "I want to go to the mountain.

Jack turned to her in amazement. "To the *mountain*?" he gasped.

Suddenly, Laura seemed to come down to earth again. "What?" she said to Jack, confused.

"You said you wanted to go to the mountain," said Peggy, stopping her writing.

"Did I?"

The children looked at each other. Laura was as bewildered by her behaviour as the others. What could be happening to her? She just felt compelled, somehow, to go to the mountain, but she didn't really know why. And she somehow knew that they needed to move on – and soon. It was almost as if she could sense the stealthy movements of the Silverskulls as they made their way, closer and closer, toward the camp.

Other titles available
in this series:

Enid Blyton's™

THE SECRET MOUNTAIN

5

Screenplay novelisation
by Gillie Russell

Collins
An imprint of HarperCollins*Publishers*

For further information on Enid Blyton™ please contact
www.blyton.com

Original Screenplay by Rio Fanning.

This screenplay novelisation first published
in Great Britain by Collins 1998
Collins is an imprint of HarperCollins*Publishers* Ltd
77-85 Fulham Palace Road, Hammersmith,
London, W6 8JB

1 3 5 7 9 8 6 4 2

Copyright © Enid Blyton Ltd 1998
All rights reserved. Developed from the TV script
which is © Cloud 9 Screen Entertainment.

Enid Blyton's signature mark and Mystery and Adventure
are trademarks of Enid Blyton Ltd.

ISBN 0 00 675315 9

The author asserts the moral right to
be identified as the author of the work.

Printed and bound in Great Britain by
Caledonian International Book Manufacturing Ltd,
Glasgow G64

CHAPTER ONE

A plane landed at the tiny airport of Boluto, bumping on the rough ground in the early morning sun. It was being watched from the airport building by Oliver West, a retired pilot in his late fifties. As the door of the plane opened and the steps were wheeled into place, Oliver saw the family he had come to meet standing at the top. There were two women, a man and four children.

"Back on terra firma, Ruby. Safe and sound, eh?" said the man, starting to walk down the steps.

Ruby, who looked after Thaddeus Arnold's children whenever he went on his expeditions, shuddered as she walked towards the small airport hut. "Never again!" she groaned. "Never again will I go up in that thing!"

Jack, the eldest of the children, and Thaddeus's adopted son, grinned at her. "It was great, Ruby. Didn't you think so?"

"Great?" she gasped. "You're joking! If we were supposed to fly, we'd have wings!"

The children's dog, Prince, a beautiful brown and white collie, barked once, looking up at her.

"See?" said Ruby. "Even the dog agrees with me." Laura, Peggy and Mike looked at each other and giggled.

Oliver West came forward to greet them as they passed through the tiny Customs post of Boluto Airport.

"Mr Arnold?" he asked, and held out his hand. "I'm Oliver West. I've got your Land Rover for you," he went on, gesturing to where it was parked.

"Excellent," said Thaddeus, shaking Oliver's hand. "Thank you."

"I've read a lot about you," said Oliver, "but I didn't think I'd ever get to meet the famous explorer in person."

Thaddeus smiled and brushed aside the compliment with a wave. "Thank you," he said again, and turned to introduce his companion. "This is Charlotte..."

"Charlie," she insisted, smiling at Oliver.

"And my brood," Thaddeus went on. "Laura, Jack, Mike, Peggy. And Ruby," he said, patting her arm.

"I'm not his brood," she protested, grinning.

"Just brooding about flying," said Peggy, the elder of the two girls, her long fair hair tied into plaits and a pink scarf tied gypsy-like on her head.

"You don't like flying then, Ruby?" asked Oliver. She shuddered. "Well, join the club! Are you going to be away for long?" he said, turning back to Thaddeus. All Oliver knew was that the Arnolds were going to trek through the jungle to see an ancient statue buried deep in the forest. They needed the Land Rover to take them the first part of the way.

"Oh, just for a few days and then, well... I've got to be back," replied Thaddeus absentmindedly. "Some appointment I've got to keep. Now... what *was* that?" he said, looking worried.

"Dad, you're hopeless!" said Peggy.

"Well, give me a clue, then. Jog my memory."

"Confetti," said Jack.

"Confetti?" Thaddeus looked puzzled.

"Ding-dong?" said Laura, the younger girl, peering at her father through her glasses.

"Bell?" prompted Jack, grinning at him.

"Pussy's in the well?" Thaddeus smiled back.

"Ring!" said Jack in despair.

"Oh, yes, of course." Thaddeus nodded. "We're getting married." And he smiled at Charlie.

She and the children laughed. Thaddeus was good at teasing.

"Congratulations," said Oliver.

"Right!" said Thaddeus, keen to get on with the trip. "Who wants to be map-reader?"

"Me!" cried Jack, taking the map from his

outstretched hand.

Thaddeus turned to the others. "So, everyone ready?"

"Yes!" they all shouted enthusiastically. This was the day they'd been looking forward to for ages.

"Mosquito guns stowed?" he asked, grinning at Peggy.

"Yes," she said.

"Elephant repellent applied?" he asked Laura.

"Yes," she smiled at her father.

"Then what are we hanging around for? An ancient and mysterious statue awaits us in the mountains. Mount up!"

The children cheered as they headed towards the Land Rover. Their jungle adventure was about to begin!

CHAPTER TWO

The full moon shone eerily on the mountain of Caldera, not far from Boluto. Inside, in a temple carved out of the very mountain itself, a mysterious ceremony was taking place. As the moon began to cast its light through the roundel window, it fell on the masked face of a goddess.

An echoing voice rang through the cave. The High Priest, wearing a hideous, skull-like mask, neither human nor animal, and surrounded by bowing acolytes, was chanting. The acolytes were of two types: some were giant figures, wearing jaguar-head masks; the others wore huge silver skulls. They were all moving in a dangerous and threatening way to the chanting of their High Priest.

"The moon approaches the sacred ring..." he chanted, and the Silverskulls sat down in circles, facing the high altar.

"...The time has come for the tribe to be reborn..." wailed the High Priest, and the Silverskulls clapped their hands above their heads and then threw themselves full-length on to the flat volcanic floor.

In the centre of the temple, surrounded by a wooden parapet and decorated with sacred symbols, was a dark and ominous-looking well covered with a wooden lid. Steam hissed through the cracks of the lid, sending clouds around the terrifying faces of the Silverskulls.

Above the well a strange cage was hanging, and inside was a masked man, his face painted in red and white.

At another altar sat the goddess, dressed in a flowing white gown, her face a ghostly mask. She watched the mysterious movements of the people on the floor in front of her.

Slowly, the lid of the well began to rise. Steam hissed out, sending huge clouds jetting to the ceiling. Now the sacred cage, with its human sacrifice, sank down towards the gaping hole – and disappeared.

The High Priest raised his arms to the moon as its beams fell on the face of the goddess. "…Soon the moon will reveal the new goddess," he intoned, and the goddess watched her silently from the altar.

Thaddeus, Charlie, the children, Ruby and Prince set out in the heavily-laden Land Rover, their spirits high and their excitement growing at the thought of what lay ahead of them.

They drove towards Mount Caldera, the climb getting steeper and more difficult by the minute. The Land Rover, though built to handle such difficult terrain, began to labour as they crossed a river and headed up into the jungle.

The scenery was breathtaking and the children were silent as they looked out at its strange and mysterious beauty. None of them had ever seen anything quite like it before. They couldn't wait to start their trek on foot when they reached the end of the track.

Thaddeus had told them so much about the jungle and the statue in the mountains that they'd thought about nothing else for weeks. At least this was one advantage of having a father who was an explorer, though they didn't like not seeing him for ten months of the year!

At last the Land Rover could go no further. Thaddeus pulled up and turned round.

"Right, this is the end of the road. For four wheels, anyway. Everyone out."

As the others jumped down, Charlie looked out of the window. "Where are the guides, Thaddeus?"

"Well, they're supposed to be here. Unless we got it wrong."

Charlotte got out of the Land Rover. "How can we have got it wrong?" she said, puzzled. "This is the end of the trail."

Thaddeus ignored her and started to organise everyone. "Right, kids, get your rucksacks."

The children swarmed up to the car. As Laura turned round with her sleeping-bag and rucksack, she saw two native men watching them from the bush at the side of the track. She tugged at her father's sleeve and nodded in their direction.

"Dad," she said quietly.

"Yeah?" he replied, busy in the back of the car. And then something in his daughter's tone made him turn round. Everyone fell silent at the sight of the two men standing proudly, holding their spears and staring back at them fiercely.

"Ah," said Thaddeus. "These will be them. I hope," he added.

He walked towards the two figures, with Prince barking at his side. The younger man immediately pointed the head of his spear towards the dog.

"Prince! That's enough!" shouted Thaddeus, and the young man turned his spear upwards once more as Prince quietened down.

"*Jambo. Habari,*" said Thaddeus to the older man.

"*Sanu. Yawa,*" he replied.

"Don't mind the dog," Thaddeus said, holding Prince by the scruff of the neck. "He's quite harmless. Your name?" he asked.

"Huaman," said the man.

"Chauca," said the other.

"Thaddeus," said Thaddeus, pointing at his chest. "And this is Jack, Laura, Charlie, Mike. And Peggy."

Chauca and Peggy smiled at each other, almost as though they shared some common bond.

"Are you the ones taking us to the statue?" she asked them.

The young man nodded and turned to walk away into the forest.

"Come on, then, everyone. Quickly, quickly," called Thaddeus, concerned that they wouldn't keep up with their guides.

"You'll be all right?" he asked Ruby, who was staying behind with Prince.

"Of course," she said, smiling at him.

"Now don't forget to tell the vicar to book the venue..." he said mysteriously. "And remember to pick up my wedding clothes."

"It'll be taken care of, don't worry. You have a wonderful time, and I'll see you the day after tomorrow."

"Thanks," said Thaddeus gratefully, hurrying after the others.

Ruby turned to Prince. "Come on, Prince. Come on, boy." And Prince jumped into the front seat of the Land Rover. "Although why they want to go and see a stupid old statue, I don't know."

Ruby climbed in the driver's side and slammed the door. "Come on, let's get back to civilisation," she said. "I think this jungle's a bit too creepy for me."

Far away from where Thaddeus, Charlie and the children were, and deep in the jungle, the strange sound of chanting could be heard. From a sacred area near the mountain a band of terrifying Silverskulls suddenly rushed out from the bush and on to the forest trail.

Further down the mountain, in a clearing in the forest, as the sound of chanting rose to a crescendo, a mysterious creature materialised from the trees around her. She appeared to be human, but on her head and growing out of her fingers were the exotic feathers of a bird. As the chanting in the distance rose for the second time to a crescendo, the Birdwoman held out her arm and a white cockatoo with yellow head feathers flew down and landed on it.

"Soon this evil will end," she said, her voice musical and slow. "I see people coming from afar."

Her face was lit by the moonlight. "We will protect them," she sang out. The cockatoo flew off as silence fell around her.

CHAPTER THREE

The children were settling down into a rhythm now that their legs had become used to the climb. Huaman went first, with Chauca bringing up the rear. The two guides took them through the dense forest along a path no one could see.

Once, at a fork in the trail, Chauca left the track and returned a few moments later holding a beautiful orchid, his brown eyes shining with pleasure. Because he was at the back, no one noticed.

"Let's take a breather," called Thaddeus a little later, seeing his children were beginning to flag.

"Anyone want a peppermint?" offered Charlie.

"Yes, please!" everyone answered.

"Thanks," said Thaddeus, looking round him to get his bearings.

The children sucked on their sweets, enjoying the rest. Chauca made his way over to Peggy with the beautiful orchid in his hand.

He held the flower out to her. "From Chauca," he said, smiling.

"Thank you," she said, surprised and pleased, though not sure what she'd done to deserve this.

"Sweetie papers, please," called Thaddeus, gathering them up from the children. "We don't want to litter the bush."

Laura, looking pensive and rather disgruntled, turned to her sister. "Why didn't he give me a flower, too?" she asked.

"'Cause your head isn't big enough," teased Jack.

"Thanks a lot, Jack!" said Peggy, secretly glad that Jack had brought the whole episode down to earth.

Thaddeus took the sweet wrapper from Laura, but didn't notice when one of the wrappers fell from his hand and drifted to the forest floor.

Ruby was busy negotiating the Land Rover back down the rough trail through the forest, with Prince beside her. He looked out through the windscreen as she drove towards the river they'd crossed on their way up the track.

She steered carefully and steadily through the water but, just before she reached the opposite bank, the Land Rover lurched violently over a rock and stalled.

"*Now* what?" groaned Ruby.

She looked out of the driver's window and saw to her dismay that the rear wheel was firmly stuck in the mud.

"Oh, no!" she wailed. "That's all I need. Stuck

in the mud in Bolo-Bolo land!"

Far away from Ruby and Prince, deep in the jungle, the party of Silverskulls was moving stealthily through the trees.

As the children, Charlie and Thaddeus trekked on through the forest, Huaman, leading the group up the trail Indian-file, stopped and looked warily at Mount Caldera through a gap in the trees. It seemed strangely ominous.

"Come!" he said suddenly, gesturing away from it.

"No, wait," Thaddeus said, getting out his compass. Jack peered over his shoulder and saw the needle swing right round towards the mountain.

"That's weird," he said.

"Fascinating," said Thaddeus. "I wonder if we go near it."

"I hope not," Charlie said emphatically. "It gives me the creeps."

Thaddeus laughed. "It's only a mountain."

"I don't like it either, Dad," said Laura, her face worried.

"Huaman," said Thaddeus, "what is that mountain? Can we take a closer look at it?"

Huaman surprised them by his reaction.

"No!" he cried out violently.

His anxiety seemed to spread itself to the others. "Thaddeus, let's leave it. This *is* supposed to be the children's treat," said Charlie.

"We can still see the statue," Thaddeus replied, looking over at the mountain again. "Huaman, how much time would it add to the journey?"

"No!" said Huaman again. "*Hapana masuri*. Not good."

"Thaddeus!" implored Charlie.

"Oh, all right." Thaddeus gave in – there was no point in having an argument about it. And Charlie was right. He had promised the children that this was their special adventure, not his. He gestured to Huaman to lead on, and they started up the forest track once more.

"Chauca?" whispered Jack, curious. "Why wouldn't Huaman go near the mountain?"

"Evil god live there," said Chauca. "Evil spirits."

"He could be right." Peggy shuddered a little. "It looks evil to me!"

Almost as if it heard them, the mountain seemed to rear up again through the next gap in the trees.

"You don't believe all that, do you?" Jack asked Peggy.

"Chauca does," said Mike. "Anyway, I'm glad

I'm not going there."

Further up the mountain track, and heading down towards Thaddeus and his party, the terrifying figures of the Silverskulls crept silently through the trees, getting closer and closer.

Laura was feeling tired. Her legs were aching and she couldn't wait for Thaddeus to find a place where they could stop and eat something.

Peggy felt the same. "I want to stop for a rest, I'm hungry," she said, her rucksack bumping uncomfortably on her back.

"Me too," said Jack.

Chauca appeared unexpectedly at their side.

"Chauca's back again," said Laura.

"I didn't even know he'd gone," Jack muttered.

Chauca, standing in front of Peggy, was offering her some strange-looking fruit. "Eat!" he urged her.

"Looks funny," said Peggy, staring at the bumpy yellow fruit Chauca had thrust into her hands.

"Eat!" said Chauca again.

Tentatively, Peggy bit into it. After a moment or two, a delighted smile spread across her face. "Oh, it's lovely. It tastes fantastic!" she cried.

"What about us?" asked Mike, feeling left out.

"Peggy first," replied Chauca. "Now you." And he distributed the rest of the fruit.

They walked on again, all thinking how well Chauca understood the bush. Not only did he know where to find beautiful orchids, he knew what to eat when you were feeling exhausted. They were beginning to realise that Chauca was someone quite special.

"So, Chauca, what's the name of your tribe?" asked Jack, echoing the thoughts of the others.

"Tracker," replied Chauca.

"Is it a big tribe?" asked Peggy.

"Once," said Chauca. "Now just Huaman, Chauca. And Ayala."

"Who's Ayala?" asked Mike.

"My friend," said Chauca, looking serious. "Girl."

"Just the three of you?" Peggy couldn't quite believe that there could really be a tribe with only three people in it.

"Yes," said Chauca, and his face suddenly looked sad.

"Why's that?" asked Jack.

"All dead. Evil god. In mountain." Chauca almost spat the words out in his distress.

"In the mountain?" Peggy was really curious now.

"Evil spirits, killed all Trackers," Chauca added.

"Oh, I am sorry. And... thanks for the fruit," she said, wanting to say something kind to him, "and the flower," she added shyly.

Jack took a bite of the fruit Chauca had given him, but he didn't like it. He made a face and let it fall to the ground.

"That's terrible about Chauca's tribe, isn't it, Dad?" Peggy said, catching up with her father.

"Yes, it is, Peggy. But it's much more likely to be disease than evil spirits that killed them." Thaddeus was nothing if not realistic.

"Well, I still think it's very sad," she said.

CHAPTER FOUR

Behind, on the forest trail, the Silverskulls were gaining on them, sliding like ghosts through the trees, getting closer and closer to the children.

One of them stopped abruptly and bent down to pick something up from the track. It was a sweet wrapper, the white paper glowing luminously in the shadows. Turning round, he waved it at the other Silverskulls. Nodding their heads slowly, they continued in the same direction as the Arnold family group.

Thaddeus, Charlie and the children trudged wearily behind their guides. Suddenly Huaman stopped, the others almost colliding with him on the trail. Ahead of them through the trees they could see the mountain again.

"What's the matter?" whispered Jack.

"The mountain," answered Chauca.

"What about it?" Jack was impatient to get on.

Huaman pointed suddenly down a narrow track in the opposite direction from the mountain. "Come!" he ordered them.

Thaddeus frowned. "How strange! I thought we had been moving away from it anyway."

"So did I," said Charlie. "So did Huaman, by the look on his face."

Thaddeus got out his compass again. The needle swung immediately in the direction of the mountain once more.

Ruby was desperate. She had just finished putting some small branches under the back wheels of the Land Rover in an attempt to stop them from skidding on the muddy river bed when she tried to drive it out.

She climbed back into the driver's seat, Prince looking agitated and turning round and round next to her. After a couple of goes the engine started. Ruby let off the hand brake, ready to ease the Land Rover out of the river bed. The engine roared – and the wheels spun. It was no use; she was stuck fast.

Back on the jungle trail, a white cockatoo watched the children from a tree as they appeared below him. One by one they passed underneath the tree – but no one noticed him, except Laura. She stopped as she passed and looked up.

"Look, everyone, there's a parrot!" she said delightedly.

But the rest of her family showed no interest.

"Yeah, great," said Jack, his mind set on what he was going to eat when they made camp.

"Oh, yeah, I see it," said Peggy, too weary to

be very interested.

"Come on, Laura!" called Thaddeus.

But Laura dawdled on the track, reluctant to leave the bird. "'Bye," she said after a moment, and waved at the parrot as she turned to go. She was about to start after the others when, with a whirring of wings, the cockatoo dropped right down on to her shoulder. Laura screamed, surprised and delighted at the same time.

"Isn't he beautiful?" she called to the others. "He just flew down on to my shoulder. Gave me a fright, though."

"Laura!" called Thaddeus. "Will you please keep up with us!"

Charlotte turned back to Laura and began to stroke the beautiful white bird.

"It's so tame," she said to Laura.

"It's lovely, isn't it?" said Peggy, joining them.

"I'm going to call him Snowy," said Laura, her eyes shining behind her glasses. She loved all wildlife.

"Hey, nobody's going to have it. It belongs to the wild," said her father, turning round.

"Aw, Dad, please!" pleaded Laura.

Thaddeus hesitated. "All right. Huaman says we're about five minutes away from a good resting place. But then the cockatoo goes. Understood?"

"Yes, I suppose you're right," agreed Laura. As they set off on the track again, something made Laura look up once more.

It was a Birdwoman, almost completely camouflaged by the trees, her feathers blending in with the foliage. Laura hesitated in disbelief. She must be seeing things because she was tired; this jungle had a strange effect on her, she thought. Then, shaking her head, she walked on.

High in the tree, the Birdwoman folded her feathered arms over her face.

Huaman and Chauca led them all to a good resting place by a stream and lit a fire. Everyone settled down beside it to eat their lunch.

"Now, go easy, everyone," Thaddeus warned them. "There's a long way to go yet. If you eat everything now, you'll go without later."

"What about Chauca and Huaman?" asked Peggy. "Should we share our food with them?"

"Oh, I think you'll find they're all right," smiled Thaddeus knowingly.

"But they didn't bring anything to eat, they were just carrying their spears," said Mike, bewildered.

"Go and see," said his father, nodding in their direction.

The children trotted over to the fire where

Huaman and Chauca were spearing large white grubs on to the end of twigs and sticking them in the fire. After a few moments of cooking, they popped the grubs into their mouths. The children were speechless. They'd never seen anything quite so disgusting, and it showed on their faces. Chauca turned to Peggy, offering her a grub. It was all she could do not to scream with disgust.

"No, thank you!" she said vehemently.

Chauca turned to Jack and offered it to him on the end of his stick.

"It's like a giant maggot," said Jack, fascinated.

"You mean they're actually eating *maggots*?" Mike thought the whole idea revolting.

"Grubs," corrected Charlotte.

"How can they be eating *grubs*?" murmured Laura in horror.

"They're hungry!" laughed Charlie.

"They're like nibbles at a party," grinned Thaddeus.

Peggy shuddered. "I could *never* eat a grub!"

"It's a different culture, that's all," explained Thaddeus. "They'd find some of the stuff we eat very peculiar. Grubs are a high source of protein. It's very necessary in a world like this. It's their idea of fast food, really."

Listening to Thaddeus, Jack took a tentative bite out of the grub, watching Chauca casually munching on his.

"Remember, if you're hungry enough, you'll eat anything," said Thaddeus.

Jack had turned rather green. "I don't think I want to eat at all now," he gulped.

"Don't be silly," said Charlotte.

As the children munched their food, the cockatoo flew down to the ground close to them. He picked up Laura's red plastic spoon in his beak and flew off again into the trees.

Laura stood up. "Wait! Here! Please come back!" she called to the bird, running after him.

The cockatoo, carrying Laura's spoon in its beak, flitted ahead of her from branch to branch. Laura stumbled on, desperate not to lose sight of Snowy, as she'd christened him. The others didn't even notice her leave the fireside.

Not far away, the Silverskulls threaded their way through the trees, hot on the heels of Huaman, Chauca and the others.

CHAPTER FIVE

Thaddeus, Charlie and the children were resting by the stream, feeling refreshed after their break and looking forward to reaching the statue.

Suddenly, Peggy looked round. "Where's Laura, Dad?"

"I've no idea," he said, getting up. "I thought she was with you lot."

"Maybe she went after that bird," said Charlotte, getting up and stretching her limbs.

Thaddeus began to look worried. "Laura!" he called.

Laura was still chasing the cockatoo. Something about the bird made it irresistible to her, and he had her camping spoon, too. But she didn't realise she was getting further and further away from her family.

Puffing and panting from her efforts to keep up, Laura ran out of the trees into a clearing, stumbling after Snowy. "Wait!" she called. "Come back with that! I need it!"

The bird flew to a wooden pole erected in the clearing. Looking at Laura, he dropped the spoon on to the leafy ground in front of her. Laura froze.

In the centre of the clearing stood the mysterious Birdwoman she thought she'd glimpsed earlier. This strange figure drew closer to Laura, and began to dance – a rhythmic, hypnotic dance – looking deeply into Laura's eyes. As she spoke, her voice seemed to echo through the forest around them.

"Peace, my child," she said. "Peace. Do not be frightened."

"Wh–what do you want?" stammered Laura.

"Listen. Listen. You must take care. Danger..." the Birdwoman intoned.

And into Laura's mind came an image of some terrifying-looking people, wearing masks and carrying burning torches. *"Danger?"* she gasped.

"Evil." The Birdwoman's voice echoed through the trees.

Another image flashed through Laura's mind. This time it was of someone who looked like a priest, and in front of him was a kind of cage which was being lowered into... the scene went, and Laura's mind felt like a misty cloud.

"Evil approaches you. Danger..." the Birdwoman repeated her message in her resonant voice.

"Danger?" whispered Laura. "What sort of danger?" And again, as if the Birdwoman was communicating straight into Laura's mind, she saw a dream-like vision of fiery skulls and then the mysterious mountain looming in the background. She tried to get rid of the scary picture, shaking her head.

"You must take care. Beware. Thorns... "

And Laura saw men with huge silver skull-like heads blowing poison darts at... at what? The picture changed.

"Chains…" intoned the Birdwoman.

This time Laura saw a dream-like picture of her family, chained and shackled together like prisoners.

"Boiling water…" the Birdwoman's voice was beginning to make Laura feel faint, and she could see a female, robed and masked, near clouds of smoke or steam.

"I don't understand…" Laura was feeling dizzy with the images in her mind.

"Believe in the bird. The bird will protect you," said the Birdwoman, and the cockatoo fluttered on his pole.

"Close your eyes…" soothed the voice of the Birdwoman.

"The cockatoo…" murmured Laura faintly.

"Close your eyes. You have things to do. Miles to go before you wake. We are in your hands."

Laura's eyes closed, as if in some kind of trance, and the cockatoo shrieked on its perch.

Thaddeus was getting very worried now.

"Laura!" he called urgently.

"Laura!" echoed Jack.

Chauca began studying the ground, looking for her tracks. At last he pointed a way through the trees. "Here!" he called to them, and he beckoned. Thaddeus and the others followed him, away from their peaceful resting place, into the jungle.

Chauca looked carefully, scrutinising every leaf and broken twig for signs. The others, following Chauca through the dense forest, were frightened now, worried that Laura was truly lost. The forest was so huge.

"Laura!" called Peggy desperately, her high voice spiralling through the treetops.

"Laura!" Jack shouted, his voice cracking.

"Lau-ra!" Thaddeus and Charlie called out in unison.

Soon Chauca reached the clearing where the Birdwoman had been. There was Laura, alone and sitting peacefully, as if in a trance.

Thaddeus approached her quietly, sensing something had happened and not wanting to scare her. The children followed him.

He knelt down beside his daughter. "Laura?" he called softly.

She didn't reply.

"Laura, darling," he repeated.

And Laura turned her head, looking straight at her father and said, as if nothing had happened, "Oh, hello, Dad. Are you ready to move on now?"

"Are you all right?" They all heard the concern in Thaddeus's voice.

"Yes," said Laura. "Just feel a little bit sleepy, that's all." And she rubbed her eyes.

The children looked at each other. Laura sounded normal, but she didn't look it. Thaddeus held out his hand to help her up.

"How did I get here?" Laura asked him, staring round the clearing.

"Can't you remember?" asked Charlotte, putting her hand on Laura's shoulder, concerned.

Laura looked thoughtful. "Snowy had my spoon…"

Mike picked the spoon up from the ground. "Here it is!" he called to them.

"Well, if you're all right," said Thaddeus, "shall we get moving again?"

Laura nodded.

"Good," said her father. "Come on, everyone." And they all started back through the clearing the way they had come.

Suddenly, the cockatoo flew down and landed

on Laura's shoulder.

"Hello, Snowy," said Laura, as though it were perfectly normal for him to be back with her again. But she remembered nothing about the Birdwoman at all.

Further up the mountain trail, the Silverskulls had found the fruit that Jack had discarded. They looked at each other and then headed off through the trees, following the family once more in a threatening, shadowy group.

CHAPTER SIX

Thaddeus and his children returned to the resting place in silence. They started to gather up their gear, ready to move on. There was an air of preoccupation about as they sorted their things, feeling rather downcast after Laura's strange disappearance.

"What do you think really happened?" Charlotte asked Thaddeus, away from the children's hearing.

"I've no idea," he said.

"Is it possible she lost her memory for a minute? Perhaps she's overtired?"

"I don't know, Charlie," said Thaddeus, not wanting to make too much of the incident. "Laura!" he called. "Remember, that bird stays behind."

"Oh, Dad!" begged Laura.

"No argument!" Her father was adamant.

"But he was given to me!" she beseeched him.

"What on earth do you mean, he was *given* to you?" Thaddeus was bewildered by his daughter's behaviour.

"I don't know," she said, "it just *feels* like he was."

"Laura," said Thaddeus, his patience running out, "stop fantasising. Leave it where it is."

"Your dad's right, Laura. You know it's time to let it go," said Charlie, trying to take the sting out of Thaddeus's words.

Quietly, Chauca came up behind Laura. He reached out to the cockatoo. "I take," he said gently. But as he took the bird it flew away from him and came to rest on a nearby branch – a branch with fronds and feathers around it. For an instant, Laura thought it might be that strange Birdwoman again...

Huaman nudged Chauca. "Go!" he called out.

And without another word, Chauca led the way along the bank of the stream to a suitable fording place.

Standing in the water, Thaddeus splashed his face – the jungle was hot and the mountain water felt wonderfully cool. He dried his face on his neck scarf, feeling refreshed. The others were doing the same, cooling themselves in the sparkling water. Chauca nudged Laura.

"What?" she asked, turning to him.

Chauca pointed to a tree close by. It was the cockatoo. "Bird," he said.

"Oh, yes!" breathed Laura. "Don't let Dad see it," she whispered to him.

Peggy splashed over to her sister. "What really happened back there?" she asked.

"I don't know," Laura murmured, "I had a

dream, I think."

"What sort of dream?" Jack sounded irritated and curious at the same time. Laura often had strange feelings about places and things. Mostly they irritated him, but very often she was right about them.

"I think I saw a woman, with feathers all round her face," said Laura. "She was very strange-looking, but she wasn't frightening," she added.

Chauca, listening nearby, looked startled. "Birdwoman," he said emphatically. "Did she speak?"

"*Sort* of," said Laura. "I could hear words in my head. Pictures, really."

"What sort of pictures?" asked Chauca.

"I saw rocks... and boiling water... and men with canes, and a big thorn," she remembered.

"Birdwoman!" cried Chauca. "She good!" And up in the trees the cockatoo sat watching them.

"Come on, you lot!" Thaddeus was eager to get moving again. "We'll never get to the statue at this rate. Let's get going!"

The group gathered themselves together and set off from the other bank, on the move once more, with Huaman in the lead.

The trees were beginning to thin as he took

them out of the denser part of the forest. Suddenly Huaman stopped dead in his tracks, as if frozen.

"Back!" he ordered.

"Back? What do you mean 'Back'?" said Thaddeus crossly.

In the distance the eerie mountain towered above them.

"Home!"

"Home? But what about the statue? We haven't seen the statue yet!" Thaddeus was getting angrier and more confused by the minute.

"Home! Go home!" repeated Huaman.

"Look, I promised the kids a treat," reasoned Thaddeus, trying to calm everything down.

In the branches, the cockatoo watched the group, fluttering his wings.

"No! No, go!" Huaman said again. And he started to walk back the way they had come.

Thaddeus turned to Chauca. "What's the matter with him?" he asked.

"Evil spirits draw us to the mountain," Chauca murmured.

"Tell him to move on." Thaddeus had lost patience.

"He won't go," said Chauca.

"Well, you take us, then," ordered Thaddeus.

"No." Chauca shook his head.

"Thaddeus, listen to them! I've got a feeling they're right," said Charlie. Something was making her feel anxious – very anxious not to go on.

"What *are* you saying?" Thaddeus turned to her in surprise.

"I'm nervous," said Charlie.

"Oh, Charlie. It's just a mountain. A forest. And some bird cries," Thaddeus said stubbornly.

"I think we should go back," Charlie insisted.

"The kids don't want to go back. Do you?" he asked, turning to his children. "After all, we've come all this way."

They looked at each other, embarrassed.

"I'd like to go on," said Jack, not wanting to upset Thaddeus.

"Me, too," said Mike, not wanting to be shown up by Jack.

There was a silence.

"Peggy?" asked Thaddeus after a while. "What about you?"

"I don't know…" said Peggy, looking awkward.

"Laura?" Thaddeus turned in desperation to his younger daughter.

"Go home!" There was no doubt at all about what Laura wanted to do.

"Oh, Laura, you are so *wet*!" said Jack.

"OK, Jack, that's enough." Thaddeus could see things were getting out of hand.

"I think we should vote on it," said Charlie, always the person to be fair.

"The two boys want to go on. The girls don't. What's the point?" Thaddeus grumbled.

Really, Thaddeus could be more childish than his own kids at times, thought Charlie. "Let's have a vote, Thaddeus," she said again.

"OK, you win," he said, giving in. "Hands up all those in favour of trekking on to see the statue."

Thaddeus raised his hand, then Jack. But no one else did.

"Mike!" said Thaddeus. "I thought you wanted to go!"

"I do, but—" Mike looked unhappy and torn.

"All those in favour of going back?" asked Charlie.

Slowly, all the others raised their hands. Thaddeus and Jack were outvoted.

"Right, you win," said Thaddeus, his ill-humour gone.

"Sorry, Dad," said Peggy.

Thaddeus looked at his watch. "OK. Now, it's too late in the day to turn back – we'll make camp for the night and go back in the morning."

With a feeling of relief, the children turned to

each other, sensing that they'd made the right decision.

High in the trees, the white cockatoo watched them, his head outlined against the mountain looming in the background.

"It's no use, Prince!" cried Ruby desperately, revving the Land Rover's engine again to no avail. "It looks like you and me are stuck here for the night."

Prince licked her face comfortingly.

Ruby put her arm round the dog. "I'm so glad you're with me," she said into his warm fur. "We're going to be all right, aren't we?"

CHAPTER SEVEN

The moon began to glint eerily on the Silverskulls as they approached Thaddeus's camp through the dense forest. They were gaining on the children, minute by minute.

"I was looking forward to seeing that statue," said Jack as he sat with the other children at a small camp fire, a little way away from Thaddeus and Charlotte's site.

"So was I," Mike said, staring into his mug of cocoa.

Jack rounded on him. "Well, why didn't you vote then?" he demanded.

"I did vote," replied Mike truthfully. "The first time." He didn't say any more, not wanting to get into an argument with Jack. They were all tired.

Peggy was sitting writing, bringing her diary up to date by the light of the fire, and Laura seemed still to be in a daze.

"I don't care about the statue," said Peggy. "I'm much happier to be going back, anyway."

"I feel… I feel…" Laura murmured distantly.

"What?" asked Peggy, without looking up from her diary.

"I feel… I want to go on." The moonlight was reflected on Laura's glasses, adding to her faraway look.

"Well, why did you vote to go back, then? What are you two playing at?" Jack was exasperated – he'd been really looking forward to this adventure, and it was being spoilt by the others.

"I want to go on," said Laura emphatically. "I want to go to the mountain."

Jack turned to her in amazement. "To the *mountain*?" he gasped.

Suddenly, Laura seemed to come down to earth again. "What?" she said to Jack, confused.

"You said you wanted to go to the mountain," said Peggy, stopping her writing.

"Did I?"

The children looked at each other. Laura was as bewildered by her behaviour as the others. What could be happening to her? She just felt compelled, somehow, to go to the mountain, but she didn't really know why. And she somehow knew that they needed to move on – and soon. It was almost as if she could sense the stealthy movements of the Silverskulls as they made their way, closer and closer, towards the camp.

A short distance from the children, sitting by their own small camp fire, Thaddeus and Charlotte were talking in quiet voices.

"You know," said Charlotte, "I think I might

be getting fed up with all this."

"All what?" asked Thaddeus, gazing into the flames.

"All this travelling," she said. "All this adventuring. I'm beginning to think it's time we settled down."

Thaddeus looked at her, sensing the importance of what she was saying. "Is that what you want?"

"Yeah, I do," said Charlie, nodding. "I love the kids, and I'm looking forward to being a mum to them. And I would like it if you were around, too."

"I'll be there," Thaddeus said.

"All the time, I mean." Charlie wanted Thaddeus to understand. "Not disappearing halfway round the world ten months of the year."

"Hmm," said Thaddeus. He was going to have to try and sort things out. Exploring was in his blood. It was the only thing he loved doing – that and writing books about his findings afterwards. What would he do if he gave it all up? Thaddeus gazed pensively into the flames.

Laura had been sitting by the fire, half-asleep, when suddenly she spotted the cockatoo landing on a branch near their camp.

"Snowy!" she called out delightedly, and started to run after the bird as it flitted from tree to tree ahead of her.

"Laura! Come back!" shouted Peggy, worried that Laura would get lost again.

"She shouldn't run off into the forest at night," said Mike grumpily.

"We'd better get her," said Jack, and the three of them set off after Laura.

Unaware of the children's movements from their camp a little further away, Thaddeus and Charlotte were still sitting by their fire, talking.

"Don't worry, Thaddeus," Charlie was saying reassuringly, "I won't put any pressure on you. I love you just the way you are."

Thaddeus reached out his hand to take hers and suddenly felt a sudden stinging pain.

"Ouch!" he yelped, clapping a hand to his neck. "The mosquitoes are pretty carnivorous around here!"

On the edge of their campsite, hidden in the trees, were the Silverskulls. One of them put his lips to a blowpipe for the second time.

"Argh!" cried Charlotte, clasping her arm through her thin bush shirt. "You're right!"

But before she and Thaddeus had time to say anything else, they collapsed unconscious on to the ground.

As stealthily as cats, silent and quick, the Silverskulls padded into the camp. Quickly they bundled up their hostages and began to drag them off into the forest.

Three other Silverskulls fired poisoned darts at Huaman and Chauca, too, lying asleep on the ground. They didn't stand a chance either. They were hauled up and dragged, stumbling, after the others.

The children emerged from the trees and crept back to their tents.

"I did see Snowy! I did!" Laura said to Jack, desperate for them all to believe her.

"Well, he's gone now." Jack felt tired and grumpy. He wanted to get some sleep.

"If he was there at all," said Mike, thinking his twin was being fanciful again.

"He was!" cried Laura, her voice rising.

"Sshh!" said Peggy, putting a finger to her lips. "We should be asleep. If you wake Dad, we'll all be in trouble. Get to bed. Come on, all of you, get to bed!"

Grudgingly, they turned to crawl into their tents – they knew Peggy was right. But this trip was not turning out to be what they'd expected at all.

As the children zipped themselves into their sleeping-bags, oblivious to the terrible things that had happened on the other side of their camp, the moon rose, casting its mysterious light on the forest.

CHAPTER EIGHT

Thaddeus and Charlotte were dragged through the bush, their hands bound in front of them. They were still dazed and confused, and found it difficult not to slip and slide. Thaddeus craned his neck to try and see Charlie.

"Are you all right?" he called to her.

Immediately, his guards pushed him forwards up a slope in front of them, and the two Silverskulls with Charlie pulled her more brutally along the track, not caring if she was able to walk or not.

"Yes," she gasped, wanting to reassure Thaddeus.

Her two guards dragged her forwards with a jerk and she let out a scream of pain.

"Don't do that! Don't drag her like that!" shouted Thaddeus.

He wrenched himself free and staggered back down the slope, taking his captors by surprise and knocking them aside. With his bound hands he hit out at the Silverskulls holding Charlotte.

In the confusion that followed, Huaman motioned to Chauca to escape while their guards were distracted. "*Lin da*. Go!" he called to him.

While Chauca's guard went to the aid of his friends, Chauca slipped unnoticed down a gully bank and hid. As the others were dragged forwards again, and before they had a chance to notice his disappearance, he sped off through the forest in the opposite direction.

Meanwhile Thaddeus, his mind working fast, managed to untie his neck scarf and drop it on the trail at his feet.

The Silverskulls led their prisoners, scrambling and slipping, up the steep path towards the mountain. As the peak loomed above them, the group reached a great rock carved into the side of the mountain. A Silverskull pressed a section of the rock face and it rolled aside, revealing the entrance to a tunnel. Thaddeus, Charlie and Huaman were dragged inside the mountain, and the slab of rock face ground shut behind them.

The guards pushed and shoved their captives along the tunnel. Almost immediately they came to a huge flaming pit, bridged by a single tree trunk which spun to and fro, making crossing impossible. Thaddeus and Charlie gazed at the flames, horrified, and Huaman turned his face away.

Quickly and silently, two of the Silverskulls lay on the rocky floor and grasped the spinning trunk with both hands, holding it still. Thaddeus realised that this was a form of drawbridge, built to prevent enemies from entering or leaving the mountain cave, and they were going to cross over the pit – not be thrown into its fiery depths.

He turned to try and reassure Charlie, who was cowering between her two guards, but was shoved hard in the back. He stepped forward gingerly on to the tree trunk and, trying not to look down into the pit, inched carefully to the other side. He was followed by Charlotte and Huaman.

Ahead of them, some of the Silverskulls began to run, almost hysterical now, and Thaddeus, Charlie and Huaman were dragged out of the tunnel and marched towards a prison cell. But before they reached this their eyes were caught by an awesome sight. In front of them was what looked like a High Priest, robed and masked, standing by a young goddess. She was attended by weird figures wearing jaguar-head masks. They were chanting at the moon, the light of which poured into the room through a round window, their voices rising to a blood-curdling pitch.

Unaware of Thaddeus's and Charlie's capture, the children slept snugly in their tents, exhausted by the adventures of the day before.

Peggy was the first to wake the next morning. She crawled sleepily out of her tent and looked around. How strange! She couldn't see anybody, or hear anything.

"Dad?" she called into the silence. "Dad? Charlie?"

Still silence. Peggy trotted across to the other side of the camp. Nothing. No one. There was no sign of Thaddeus, Charlie, or the guides. Frightened now, Peggy called to the others.

"Laura!" she yelled.

"Yes?" Laura's sleepy head peeped out of the bottom of the tent.

"Laura, wake up!" Peggy shouted again, a note of panic in her voice.

"What?" asked Laura, dragging herself out of the tent.

Peggy shouted at the boys. "Jack! Mike!"

The two boys heaved themselves out of their sleeping-bags and poked their heads out of their tent.

"Dad and Charlie have disappeared!" Peggy shouted to them.

Jack looked anxious. "Where are they, then? Dad! Charlie!" he called, and Mike joined in, but their cries fell onto the still morning air with no answering response.

"*Everyone*'s gone!" said Peggy.

"Where are they? Where could they have gone *to*?" gasped Jack, turning round in frantic circles, his eyes searching the campsite in disbelief.

"The mountain," said Laura, in a flat little voice beside him.

"What?" asked Mike.

And the children, suddenly stilled, stared at the mountain. It seemed to rise, ominous, magnetic and sinister, over the trees in front of them.

Ruby was sleeping soundly in the driver's seat of the Land Rover, with Prince stretched across her lap, when the morning sun hit her face. She woke up, dazed and confused.

"Where are we, Prince?" she murmured.

Prince whined in sympathy and Ruby looked out of her window at the river below and the submerged wheel. Her face fell.

"Oh, yes," she whispered. "Well, we can't stay here for ever," she said suddenly, the old Ruby appearing once more. "We've got to get help somehow!"

And Prince barked in agreement.

"Good boy, Prince," said Ruby. "You've just given me an idea." And she got out her pad and a pencil.

Deep in the forest, the Birdwoman was standing waiting in the shadows beneath the trees. Above her she heard a flapping of wings, and suddenly, flying towards her, was the cockatoo.

The Birdwoman stretched out one feathery arm and the bird landed. For a moment he sat resting on her, then flew off, carrying a yellow neck scarf in his beak.

The bird flew from branch to branch, scanning the ground beneath him, until he came to the group of children.

"Snowy!" called Laura, pointing upwards. "Look, it's Snowy!" She walked towards the cockatoo, calling his name again. The bird waited until Laura was beneath the branch he was perching on, then dropped the scarf.

"Hey," said Laura, "what's that you've got?" She picked it up. "It's Dad's neck scarf!" she called out.

"Let me see!" said Peggy, running over to her.

Peggy took the spotted scarf and the others gathered round her. "It's Dad's, all right," she said.

"Where did the bird get it?" asked Jack, looking upwards.

"What are we going to do?" said Mike.

"I think we should stay here," Peggy said practically, not wanting to get lost in the forest.

"Something might have happened to Dad," said Jack. "We *have* to find him. And Charlie."

"No!" Peggy was certain that this would be foolish.

"Well, what do you suggest, Peggy?" asked Jack. "We have to at least *try* to find them."

Peggy nodded, realising he was right. Thaddeus and Charlie might be hurt somewhere, and the bird, flying from branch to branch, could be trying to tell them something. She looked up at the cockatoo and started to follow him. Mike went after her.

"Follow the parrot?" said Jack. "She's bonkers!"

"What else can we do, Jack?" called Peggy over her shoulder. "We have to try something – we have to find Dad and Charlie, you said so yourself!"

The children stood together under the trees, their anxiety mounting.

"Where are they, then?" asked Mike desperately.

"The mountain," said Laura quietly.

And they all stared up at the mountain in the distance.

CHAPTER NINE

Chauca raced through the trees, using all the skills and knowledge of the forest that he had. In spite of his bound hands he moved surprisingly fast until he suddenly tripped on a tree root, went flying through the air and rolled over. Luckily, Chauca was acrobatic, and managed to get on his feet again swiftly. He had to keep going; he knew that the Silverskulls would have noticed his escape by now and be pursuing him, following his tracks through the trees.

As he sped on through the jungle, Chauca looked back constantly over his shoulder for any sign of them.

Laura, Jack, Mike and Peggy pushed and hacked their way through the dense undergrowth of the forest. Laura was carrying the cockatoo on her shoulder and wearing Thaddeus' neck scarf. At last they emerged into a small clearing, and paused to catch their breath.

"I hope you know what you're doing, Laura," Jack said to her.

"We've got to go to the mountain," she repeated, in a flat voice.

"I hate that mountain!" said Peggy vehemently.

"So do I," said Jack. "It's just sitting there, waiting for us, isn't it?" And they looked up at the mountain through the bushes.

"It scares me, somehow," said Peggy, shivering slightly.

"You're not the only one," admitted Jack.

"We've got to keep going, Jack!" urged Laura, turning to him.

"I know," he said. "I only said I was frightened. I didn't say I was going to stop." And he started walking again, leading the way through the dense trees and shrubs.

Sometime later, Jack was ahead of the weary group tramping along the forest trail.

"Sshh!" he said, suddenly stopping. "Listen!"

"What a terrible sound!" said Peggy, and covered her ears. "I hate it!"

The cockatoo, still perched on Laura's shoulder, began to hop around, looking agitated. What the children were hearing in the distance was the low, rhythmic chanting of the Silverskulls.

"It's coming this way!" cried Mike.

"We must hide!" Laura's voice was insistent. Mike opened his mouth to complain, but Laura went on, "Don't argue! Hide!"

Frantically, the children looked around for a safe place. They clambered into the dense undergrowth, burrowing down as far as they could to be hidden by the leaves.

They were keeping a watchful eye on the track through the forest when Jack suddenly sprang to his feet.

"Chauca!" he cried. "Here!"

Chauca, leaping along the track, stopped dead when he heard Jack's voice.

"What happened, Chauca?" Peggy asked him, emerging from her hiding place, desperate to hear news of her father and Charlie.

"The mountain!" said Chauca, his eyes looking wild. "Evil spirits!"

"Where's Dad?" asked Laura. "And Charlie?"

"Are they all right?" demanded Peggy.

The children crowded around him. "Yes! Now! But when they get to the mountain, no!" he told them. Then Chauca turned to Jack. "My hands!" he said, holding them out. "My hands!"

Quickly, Jack started to untie the bonds, his fingers fumbling with the twine. Suddenly, Chauca pulled them all down to the ground.

"Keep still!" he whispered to them hoarsely. "Evil spirits follow!" And he put a finger to his lips.

The children crouched nervously in a hollow in the undergrowth with Chauca holding out his arms protectively. Then, through the trees, they saw two Silverskulls emerge, following Chauca's tracks. They stopped suddenly, searching the ground, their blowpipes at the ready. As they approached the hollow, the children froze with fear.

Then, just as they were on the point of being discovered, the cockatoo flew from Laura's shoulder with a screech – out of the bushes and straight at the Silverskulls, distracting them at the vital moment. Then he flew off high into the trees.

The Silverskulls, startled, looked up at the bird and began loping after it into the forest.

The children breathed a sigh of relief.

"Have they gone?" whispered Mike.

"Looks like it," said Jack, standing up cautiously.

Peggy stood up, too. "Come on!" she said softly to the others. "We must go, now, before those horrible creatures come back!"

The children began to make their way forward towards the mountain again, creeping quietly and carefully through the trees, terrified in case they met more Silverskulls.

"Who *were* those things?" said Jack.

"Evil spirits!" panted Chauca.

"Whatever they were, they were not evil spirits!" said Jack. He didn't believe in such nonsense.

"They are to me," Laura breathed.

"I never want to see them again," said Peggy. She just wanted to get away from this horrible place and find her father and Charlie.

"You're not the only one," agreed Mike. "But I just wish we could eat." His stomach was feeling empty and it seemed a long time since their supper the night before.

"I go," said Chauca. "Get food." And he trotted off, bent double, through the bushes.

"Look!" said Laura, pointing to a bush. "That's the same fruit Chauca gave us yesterday."

"Yesterday?" groaned Mike. "That seems like months ago!"

Peggy was ahead of them, pushing through the bush to pick some fruit. "Ouch!" she cried suddenly. "Watch out, you lot. Those thorns are sharp!" And she moved away, sucking her hand where it was scratched and slightly bleeding.

The others began picking the fruit, more cautious after Peggy's warning, and carefully avoiding the vicious-looking thorns.

"Well, at least we know that Dad and Charlie are still alive," said Jack, trying to make them feel reassured.

"Now all we need to know is where they are," agreed Mike.

"The mountain," repeated Laura, almost to herself.

"What do those people want with them anyway?" Mike went on, hardly hearing his sister's ominous words.

Far down the mountainside, Ruby jumped down from the Land Rover, still stuck in the muddy river, and waded to the bank with Prince. She tried to persuade him to carry her rolled-up hanky in his mouth.

"Pick it up!" she coaxed. "Go on, pick it up. Hold it!" she said encouragingly.

Prince picked up the material in his mouth, carrying it with the ends sticking out on either side.

"Well, what are you waiting for?" laughed Ruby. "Go and get help!"

Prince turned and trotted into the forest, the hanky dangling from his mouth. Then he stopped and looked back at Ruby.

"Go on!" she called. "Go on, Prince! I'll be fine. Just don't get side-tracked, there's a good boy!"

And Prince turned and ran off again into the forest. Ruby looked around nervously, feeling very lonely without the dog's company. She waded back to the Land Rover, climbed up into the driver's seat and slammed the door shut. She needed a distraction, something to help pass the time.

Looking at the dashboard, she switched on the ignition, and started to fiddle with the dials on the radio. The cab was suddenly flooded with the sound of African music. Ruby started to jig around in her seat, trying to cheer herself up.

"Well, it ain't rock 'n' roll, but it's close enough!" she said to herself, her eyes on the forest where Prince had disappeared.

CHAPTER TEN

Jack, Mike and Laura were still gathering the fruit. It was certainly making them feel better; none of them had realised quite how hungry they were until they'd started eating the strange, exotic flesh.

Peggy was standing a little way off, nursing her sore hand. She wasn't looking too good. She was feeling rather dizzy and just a little faint. She rubbed her hand. Then, quite suddenly, she sank to the ground with a moan.

"Peggy!" cried Laura, who'd heard her fall.

"What's happened to her?" gasped Mike.

The three of them knelt round the prone body of their sister.

"Peggy," whispered Jack, bending forward, his face close to hers.

"Has she fainted?" asked Mike.

"Look at her hand!" cried Laura.

Peggy's hand was blue and swollen.

"How did that happen?" said Jack.

"The thorns!" said Laura, as they turned and looked at the bush where they'd been gathering the fruit.

"Do you think they're poisonous?" asked Mike, going pale.

"Looks like it," muttered Jack.

"What can we do?" Laura turned to her older brother.

"We've got to get help!" It was Mike who spoke first.

"*Where* are we going to get help?" said Jack, looking desperate.

"I don't know!" said Mike. "But we've got to do something!"

They crouched down beside Peggy's still body. Luckily, Jack had remembered to pick up the First Aid kit as they'd left their camp that morning.

"In First Aid class we were told to keep the patient warm," said Laura bossily.

"We'd better do it, then," agreed Jack.

"We should have brought sleeping-bags," said Mike.

"We didn't know, did we?" Jack was already feeling worried and he didn't need Mike to tell him what they should have done.

They put some of their clothes over Peggy, trying to keep her warm as best they could.

"Listen!" whispered Laura suddenly.

"What?" Mike never found it easy to talk quietly.

"Listen!!" ordered Laura again.

Hardly daring to breathe, the three knelt by Peggy, straining their ears to listen. Sure enough, over the faint rustle of leaves and the sounds of wildlife, they heard the pad of running feet.

"Do you think it's them?" breathed Mike.

"Sshh!" Laura was trying to make out how many feet she could hear when Chauca appeared, the bushes shaking and rustling behind him. He was carrying some fruit wrapped in a bundle of leaves.

"*Chauca!*" gasped Jack, relieved.

Chauca went straight over to Peggy and knelt down beside her.

"She pricked her hand on a thorn," explained Laura.

Chauca picked up Peggy's hand and examined it gently.

"Must heal. Must cure," he said softly.

"How?" Jack asked him.

"Medicine," replied Chauca, studying Peggy's face.

"Where will we find medicine here?" asked Mike desperately.

"I go," Chauca told them. "Jack, you come with me. Must cover." He pointed to Peggy. "Keep Peggy warm."

"Is it serious?" Jack asked him, trying not to let anyone see how worried he was.

"Will she be all right?" said Laura.

"Medicine good. Need go. Quick." So saying,

Chauca took Jack's arm, steered him across the little clearing and headed off into the trees.

Laura and Mike looked at each other, their faces full of concern. Then they turned to Peggy. As if they both knew what they had to do next, they unrolled a survival sheet from their First Aid kit and placed it over her body.

The children knew they had to keep Peggy warm, whatever happened – their father had often talked to them about survival techniques. So Mike went off into the nearby jungle and picked up as much firewood as he could carry. He came back to where Peggy was lying and lit a fire close to her.

"At least that'll keep away the wild animals while we're asleep," said Laura.

"Wild animals?" said Mike, worried. "What wild animals?" Trust Laura to go imagining things again.

"Wolves... pythons... jaguars... evil spirits... "

Mike looked at his twin's face. She really spooked him sometimes.

"I don't like this place." He shuddered. "I'm frightened."

"Don't worry, Mike, I'm just joking," said Laura, and she grinned at him, her eyes glinting behind her glasses.

"It's not funny!" he said, furious that he'd fallen for her teasing. But Laura had managed to lighten their mood and they huddled down together round Peggy and their little fire, feeling more encouraged.

Threading their way through the trees, Chauca and Jack reached a beautiful clearing. There was a stream nearby, and Chauca took Jack's arm again, nodding towards the bank on the other side.

The two of them forded the stream, and disappeared into the forest beyond, Jack hoping earnestly that Chauca knew what he was doing. They just had to find the medicine, Jack thought to himself. They just had to.

Far away from the children, Prince, looking wet and bedraggled, had reached the end of his journey. He had finally made his way to Oliver West's hut, further down the mountainside. Padding up to the door, he dropped the hanky on the step and barked. He barked again. But no one was around.

There was nothing for it but to stay there. Prince knew that he had to find help for Ruby, and this was the only person for miles around who could provide it. He settled down to wait in front of the hut.

Meanwhile, Ruby was waiting alone, too. As she sat in the Land Rover she could feel herself getting more and more tense and anxious. She'd switched the radio off and was scanning the forest in front of her, her eyes straining for a glimpse of Prince coming through the trees. But she saw nothing.

"Where are you, Prince?" she murmured. "Where are you? I don't want to stay here by myself tonight."

Ruby rolled up her window and locked the car doors. The whole place looked distinctly unfriendly.

CHAPTER ELEVEN

Inside Mount Caldera, Thaddeus and Charlotte, their wrists still bound, struggled to free themselves. When the Silverskulls had thrown them in the cell, they'd tied their bodies with rope, too.

"Oh!" Charlotte let out a huge sigh of despair. "What's happening, Thaddeus?"

"I wish I knew," he said, still trying to loosen their ropes.

"Who *are* these people?" she asked him, looking at the mysterious happenings through the bars of their cell.

"Chauca's evil spirits, I suppose," said Thaddeus. "I must apologise to him, if I ever see him again…"

With a final wrench, Thaddeus managed to wriggle free of his rope and yank his hands out of the twine. He shook his wrists gently, feeling the pain. He turned to Charlie and started to untie her too. Finally they were free, standing together in the darkness of their prison cell.

"What do they want with us?" whispered Charlie.

"I have no idea," said Thaddeus, his arm round her protectively.

"Whatever it is," she said, "it's not very good,

is it?"

Thaddeus grinned at her affectionately. "Charlie, you've got a genius for understatement." And he kissed her muddy face, not wanting to let Charlie see how alarmed he really was. If they stayed in this extraordinary place, they were in great danger. Somehow they had to escape – and fast!

As dawn broke, the fire that Mike and Laura had lit to keep Peggy warm went out, and the children were asleep.

Over the treetops, the cockatoo appeared. Seeing the children down below him, he perched on a branch a short way away, as if watching over them.

Laura was the first to stir. She rubbed her eyes underneath her glasses and sat up. Suddenly, she remembered. She heaved herself up stiffly from the damp ground and went over to Peggy.

"She looks terrible," she whispered to herself.

"How is she?" Mike was awake now too. "And where are Jack and Chauca?" he called, his eyes searching the forest.

"I don't know," said Laura. "But I hope they'll be back here soon."

Mike took the last fruit from its bundle of leaves

and broke it in two. He handed half to Laura.

"No, thanks," she sighed. "I couldn't, somehow."

They sat together, silently, by Peggy's side; they could do nothing but wait.

In the Land Rover, far away down the mountain track, Ruby was just stirring, too. Around her, the forest stood silent, threatening, remote. Ruby looked at herself in the rear-view mirror. Ugh, she thought. I wouldn't like another night like this. And she tucked a wild strand of hair back under her hat.

She sat up straight, looking at the edge of the forest again.

"Great! No dog, no food, no wedding." She looked in the mirror again, her voice changing.

"How do you do it, Miss Moore?" she said to her reflection. "Oh, years of practice," she replied to herself, bitterly.

Ruby thumped the steering wheel in desperation.

"Prince! Where *are* you?" she muttered through gritted teeth.

Almost as if he'd heard her, Prince's head lifted and his ears pricked up as he lay outside Oliver West's hut.

But he was right! He really had heard something. Oliver's truck was bumping down the track towards the hut. Prince leapt up, his tail wagging furiously.

Oliver jumped down from his cab, surprised to see Prince. "Hey! What are you doing here? Where are the others?" he asked, stroking the dog. Prince barked and Oliver noticed the hanky on the ground.

"What's this, old boy?" he said, bending down to pick it up.

Oliver unfurled the scrap of material and read the note that Ruby had put inside it. "Huh. Looks like we've got some rescuing to do, old pal," he said to Prince. "Come on, then!"

Prince barked again, happy to have found help at last. His tail wagged frantically.

Oliver walked back to his truck and Prince barked again.

"Come on, Prince," said Oliver again. "Jump in. We'll find her. No worries." And he started his engine, turned the truck round and headed back up the track towards Ruby.

Thaddeus and Charlie lay sprawled on the bare rocky floor inside their prison cell in the mountain. They were hungry and exhausted and they dozed fitfully.

Suddenly, the barred door of their cell crashed open and some of the bizarre figures in jaguar-head masks crowded in. Thaddeus and Charlotte sat up, dazed and shocked. Wasting no time, the Jaguarheads dragged them both from the cell and began hustling them down some stairs.

In all his years of exploring, Thaddeus had never seen a place like this. It looked to him as though it was indeed some kind of special temple, a holy place, lit by long, fiery torches. Glancing to one side, he noticed another flight of steps, at the top of which sat the ghost-like form of the goddess figure which they'd seen the day before, masked and seated on a throne.

Thaddeus and Charlie were pushed forwards by the Jaguarheads, and made to kneel in a pool of light in front of a third smaller flight of steps. At the top of these, on a throne carved with extraordinary shapes and symbols, sat a High Priest. He was wearing a huge and hideous mask and was one of the most frightening figures that Thaddeus and Charlie had ever seen.

Silence fell. The High Priest raised a hand and the Jaguarheads hurried away immediately to the side of the room. Thaddeus and Charlie, as they knelt on the earthy floor, could sense that this person was all-powerful. What was going to happen to them?

Then, with a voice echoing harshly, the High Priest spoke. "This is so annoying!" it said.

"*What?*" Charlotte was staggered.

"You speak English?" Thaddeus was staring, not quite believing what he'd heard.

"Of course I speak English," said the voice. Then the High Priest lifted off the great mask to reveal a rather small, mousy woman.

"Ah," she said, "that's better. You've no idea how stuffy that is."

Thaddeus and Charlotte were open-mouthed with surprise.

"You're British," she said, putting on some very ordinary-looking glasses. "I'm really sorry about all this. You should not be here. The Silverskulls are very difficult to control sometimes."

Thaddeus was taken aback. "Are you saying this has all been a mistake?" he said.

"I'm afraid so," replied the High Priestess.

"Well, thank God for that." Thaddeus shook his head, relieved.

"Yes, indeed we should," intoned the woman. "Nevertheless, I am not happy about this at all."

"I should hope not," said Thaddeus.

"I've expressly forbidden them to take foreign people prisoners," she went on.

"So why did they kidnap us?" Charlotte had eventually found her voice after the shock of seeing who the High Priestess really was.

"Ah, they get carried away," said the High Priestess. "Funny people. But, still, this complicates things. Normally I wouldn't mind, but this time they were sent out specifically to look for a *child*." She looked almost sulky.

"A *child*!" Charlotte was horrified.

"A girl," the High Priestess went on. "To take the place of the present goddess."

Thaddeus nodded. So the figure on the other throne *was* some kind of goddess. "Well, since there has obviously been some sort of mistake, you'll let us go, presumably?" he said.

"I'm sorry. I'm afraid I can't do that," said the High Priestess.

"Why *not*?" Charlotte was appalled. She didn't like this woman at all – she could sense that she was cruel.

"Take them away!" ordered the High Priestess, clapping her hands to bring the Jaguarheads back, and motioning to them to remove Thaddeus and Charlie.

"You must make the best of it, both of you," she called after them as they were hauled out of the temple back to their prison cell. With a slight dismissive shrug of her shoulders, she removed her glasses and heaved the huge and terrifying mask on to her head once more.

CHAPTER TWELVE

The engine of the truck laboured over the rough terrain, bumping and groaning its way towards the river. Oliver, with Prince in the passenger seat beside him, stared out in front of him, searching for a glimpse of the river – and Ruby.

Ruby was sitting on the Land Rover roof. She had been scanning the forest, worried out of her mind, until her eyes ached. Suddenly, in the distance, she thought she heard the faint sound of an engine. No, she was probably imagining things again, she told herself.

But she *had* heard something. She was sure of it now! Quite suddenly, Prince appeared on the edge of the forest, bounding towards her, and Oliver West's truck was coming into view behind him.

"Prince!" shouted Ruby. "You made it!" And she jumped down from the roof of the Land Rover and splashed through the river towards them.

"Hello, Ruby. Need some help?" Oliver grinned at her.

"Do rabbits eat lettuce?!" said Ruby, crouching down to hug Prince. "Oh, you two are a sight for sore eyes!"

*

Chauca and Jack crept through the thick undergrowth to the edge of the forest. Chauca grasped Jack's arm, motioning him to stop. He parted the leaves in front of them cautiously.

"What is it?" whispered Jack.

In front of them, in a clearing, was a cave guarded by an eerie semi-circle of skulls mounted on stakes, which formed a line on either side of the cave mouth.

"Skulls should not be there," said Chauca. "Something wrong. Bad."

"Is this where the medicine is?" Jack asked him.

"Yes," replied Chauca. "Pool in cave."

Jack was eager to reach it, so that they could get back to Peggy. "Come on, then, let's get it." And he started forward.

"No! Danger! No go! Bad!" Chauca held Jack's arm.

"Chauca, we've got to get the medicine. Pull yourself together." Jack felt bad saying this, but Peggy was the important one now.

"Danger! I go first," said Chauca bravely.

"What danger? You've been watching too much telly, mate," joked Jack, trying to lighten the atmosphere. He didn't want to admit that he was frightened by the skulls too.

Suddenly, a great whoosh of fire leapt out of

the mouth of the cave while they were watching. Chauca and Jack jumped out of their skins in fright.

"What was *that*?" gasped Jack.

"Dragon. *Dragonman*," whispered Chauca.

"Dragon?" Now Jack thought Chauca really was going over the top.

"Yes," said Chauca. "We go in now."

"I don't believe in dragons," muttered Jack to himself, and they began creeping cautiously towards the mouth of the cave.

"You see him?" whispered Chauca.

"No. And I don't want to see him, either," murmured Jack.

Suddenly, another great ball of flame gushed out of the cave, and Jack clutched Chauca, fearful of what was inside. When the smoke from the flames had cleared, Jack saw the Dragonman, standing in front of the cave, fire gushing from his mouth as he stood on guard.

Jack looked at Chauca. "But how are we going to get into the cave?" he said desperately.

"Dragonman chase Chauca. You get medicine," said Chauca bravely.

"I don't like it," said Jack. But he couldn't see an alternative.

"We go?" Chauca nodded urgently in the direction of the cave.

"OK," said Jack, trying to summon up his courage. "We go."

The boys crept towards the cave once more, bending low and ready for anything.

"Here we go!" said Jack.

Chauca leapt into the cave, letting out an ear-splitting, warbling cry, and then ran out again. The Dragonman, surprised, rushed out of the cave, with more fire billowing from his mouth. Chauca managed to dodge out of the way, and then began to taunt him.

Jack managed to slip into the cave unseen. He scrambled down a short tunnel and there, in the centre of the cave, was the pool that Chauca had described to him. Now he must carry out Chauca's instructions.

The medicine, as Chauca had explained, was contained in the huge mussels that lay in the water. Jack inched along the floor to the side of the pool and stretched his arm down into the freezing water.

Suddenly he was lit up by the light of the Dragonman's fire! He'd come back into the cave! Chauca, trying to distract him, dodged out of the way of the flames and shouted to Jack. "Blue shell! Blue shell! Quick!"

Kneeling on the cave floor, Jack scrabbled desperately with his fingers, searching the pool for the precious blue mussels. "I'm trying!" he called back.

Chauca made a dash around the cave, followed by the Dragonman, just as Jack's hand closed over a mussel. Quickly, he grabbed it, pulling its blue shell to the surface.

Outside the cave, the skulls on their stakes turned suddenly into fiery torches. The brightest of bright lights lit up the cave and a huge explosion rent the air. The boys, knocked out by the waves of heat, fell in a heap on to the cave floor.

The pool started to bubble and steam but Jack and Chauca lay where they had fallen, unmoving. There was no sign of the Dragonman.

After some time, Jack began to stir, then he sat up. Memory came flooding back to him. "Peggy...! Chauca!" he cried weakly.

He struggled to his feet and picked up the mussel from the floor where he had dropped it as he fell. Looking round the cave, he spotted Chauca, lying not far away, and he stumbled over to him.

"Chauca! Chauca!" Jack shook him frantically. "Chauca! Wake up! Please!" he cried.

At last, Chauca began to stir. "Wh-what?" he mumbled.

"Chauca," said Jack, "are you all right?"

"What happened?" said Chauca.

Jack began to pull Chauca to his feet. "Don't you remember? The Dragonman!" he told him.

Jack managed to get his shoulder under Chauca's arm and began to stagger down the tunnel to the mouth of the cave. But Chauca was still very dazed and finally Jack had to heave him over his shoulders and half-carry him through the tunnel and out into the clearing where the skulls were.

Gasping for breath, he let Chauca slide to the ground.

"Dragonman!" Chauca had come round and remembered the fiery encounter he had just had.

"It's OK. We're safe," said Jack. "He fell into the water and disappeared," he remembered.

"Water kills creatures like him," gasped Chauca.

"Seems like it. I got the medicine," said Jack. "Is this right?"

He showed Chauca the big blue mussel shell.

"Yes!" Chauca was delighted. He picked up a small bowl that was lying in the grass in the clearing, and turned to Jack. "Now, we must hurry. Come!"

Deep in the forest, Peggy was lying, unconscious still, and moaning occasionally. Mike and Laura sat close by, watching her pale face intently.

Where were Jack and Chauca? Laura thought. If they didn't come back with the medicine soon, perhaps it would be too late.

CHAPTER THIRTEEN

Back in their prison cell inside Mount Caldera, this time with Huaman as well, Thaddeus was working desperately on Charlotte's bonds, trying to undo them.

"I wish I knew what had happened to the children!" he said. "Where are they? Are they safe?"

"All being well, they're back at camp raising the alarm," said Charlie reassuringly. She could see how worried he was.

"Provided they can find their way back," said Thaddeus.

"Of course they can," said Charlie firmly. "They're sensible kids."

But Thaddeus wasn't convinced. "Even if they manage to find their way, nobody knows where *we* are!"

Outside their cell, they could see the Silverskulls in the light of the torches. They were bowing down in front of the altar, chanting in a terrifying way.

"Chauca would," said Charlie, turning to Thaddeus again.

"Yeah. Well, let's hope he got away. Let's hope he found the children." Thaddeus was getting very despondent. He was conscious of the ceremony in the temple beginning to build to a crescendo, and he didn't even want to think what that might mean.

The High Priestess looked on in her ghastly mask, watching the preparations for the rituals to come from her throne by the altar.

"Ahh!" breathed Charlotte. "That's a relief!"

Thaddeus had at last managed to untie her hands. "Here," he said, turning round so Charlotte could loosen his which the Jaguarheads had also re-tied.

"Ruby would have missed us by now, anyway," said Charlie. Her mind had been working all the time she'd been untying the twine.

"I suppose as long as the children are out of the way, I don't really mind what happens to us," said Thaddeus, looking bitterly at Charlie.

"Yes, I agree... up to a point," said Charlie, trying to smile a little.

"Yes, you're right," said Thaddeus. He knelt down beside Huaman and started to loosen his bonds, too.

No sooner had he spoken than the bars of their prison door crashed open, and a group of Jaguarheads loomed in. They threw Thaddeus aside and dragged Huaman out into the temple, shutting Thaddeus and Charlie inside again as they left.

"What does that mean?" asked Charlie fearfully.

It was beginning to have some dreadful meaning to Thaddeus. He watched, horrified, as Huaman was prepared, as if for some terrifying sacrifice, in front of the altar. A Jaguarhead was painting Huaman's face with strange symbols, in red and white, and the High Priestess, in her mask and full ceremonial robes, still stood watching.

All around the sacrificial area, the Silverskulls started their eerie chanting once more.

"That woman…" said Charlie, trying not to let her voice crack, "that priestess, or whatever she is – she shouldn't be part of this sort of thing!"

Suddenly, there was a commotion outside their prison bars, and two Jaguarheads barged into the cell, shoving Thaddeus and Charlie to their knees. As they knelt on the hard, bare, rocky floor, the High Priestess entered. She signalled imperiously to her Jaguarheads to leave.

As soon as they had gone, she removed her mask. "Relax! Relax!" she told them. "You don't have to be so formal now."

Thaddeus and Charlie got up stiffly from the floor, looking with dislike at the strange woman in front of them.

"I hope you don't mind me popping in like this," said the High Priestess.

"Oh, not at all," replied Thaddeus dryly. "Feel free. Any time." This woman really did take the biscuit, he thought to himself. What on earth was she playing at? How could they *stop* her 'dropping in'?

"The fact is," she went on, "I get rather starved of conversation. The natives are people of few words. It's one of the biggest drawbacks in working here."

"So why are you here, then, of all places?" asked Thaddeus, curious in spite of himself.

"Money," she said in a matter-of-fact tone.

So that was it! thought Thaddeus.

"And you can find money here?" Charlotte was dumbfounded.

"Oh, billions," said the High Priestess casually. "Lumber. Minerals. Precious metals. This part of the world is a virtual gold mine."

"So *you* eliminated the Trackers?" Thaddeus nodded, suddenly beginning to understand. He remembered what Chauca had told the children about his tribe being killed by evil spirits. So this was what was behind it!

"There was no alternative." She sniffed dismissively.

"You're the Evil Spirit of the Mountain!" Charlie was horrified.

"Oh, dear. Shocked, are we?" the High

Priestess said mockingly. "What a pity. I did hope that we might be compatible."

"How dare you do this to people!" cried Charlie, outraged.

"People? They were no more people than those masked savages are people!" the High Priestess said contemptuously. "Oh, I shan't waste any more time on you!" And she turned to go.

Then she hesitated. "Still, it's a pity, really. Gets quite lonely here. You're the first white people I've seen in twelve years. Out of curiosity, what were you doing here?"

Without thinking, Thaddeus said, "We were taking the kids to see the statue."

"*Kids*, did you say?" the High Priestess asked quickly.

Thaddeus's face fell. What was he thinking of? How could he have been so stupid as to tell her anything?

"The Silverskulls didn't bring any kids back with them. How useful." She smiled a horrible smile. "I'll send out a scouting party right away."

"We... we sent them off to join another group," added Thaddeus. "They're probably on their way right now. It's a very large party," he added rather lamely.

"Nice try," said the High Priestess, mocking

once more. "But lying is not your forte. Fear not, we'll find them – if the wild animals don't find them first."

So saying, she donned her hideous mask and swept out of the prison cell, leaving Charlie and Thaddeus looking devastated behind her.

"Oh, Thaddeus," said Charlie in a small voice. "I wish you hadn't told her about the kids."

Thaddeus had turned pale. "So do I," he said grimly.

Far away down the mountainside, Oliver had just finished pulling the Land Rover out of the river and was re-winding his winch cable.

"Right. That's it," he said to Ruby. "It's fairly easy from here back to my place. You ready?"

"Just get me out of here!" cried Ruby, relief flooding her face. Oliver nodded and started towards his truck. Ruby clambered up into the driver's seat of the Land Rover once more, Prince beside her.

"Way to go, Prince!" she cried joyfully. She couldn't believe she was finally going to get back to some civilisation.

CHAPTER FOURTEEN

Chauca had re-lit the fire with Jack. Now he placed the small bowl he had found in the Dragonman's clearing on it, with the blue mussel simmering inside. He was crouching over the fire, looking into the bowl intently, with Jack beside him.

Mike and Laura, with the cockatoo on Laura's shoulders, were sitting close by, relieved that the others were back with them.

"I hope he knows what he's doing," said Mike quietly to Laura.

"He does," said Laura confidently.

Jack turned round from the fire, surprised at Laura's definite statement. "How do you know?" he asked her.

"I just do!" Laura didn't know how to explain what she was feeling lately; she just knew she was right, that was all.

"OK, OK," muttered Jack. More of Laura's premonitions, he thought.

He looked into the little bowl as Chauca poked at the shellfish inside with a stick.

"It must not open," Chauca said.

"How do you know when it's ready, then?" Jack was puzzled.

"Colour," said Chauca. "Water goes blue."

They waited for a few moments longer, then

Chauca said, "Now!" With two sticks he lifted the bowl from the flames and emptied the water onto the ground. Jack stretched out his hand to help.

"Don't touch!" warned Chauca.

Then he quickly scraped the shellfish from the steaming puddle and went over to Peggy, lying silently on the ground.

"Her mouth," he said to Laura. "Open."

Laura leant over her sister, gently easing open her mouth.

Chauca carefully and precisely held the shellfish above Peggy's face. Then he levered the wavy edges of the shell open with his strong fingers. A trickle of blue liquid splashed into Peggy's mouth, held firmly by Laura.

When all the liquid from inside the shell had been given to Peggy, he stood up. "Now we wait," he said solemnly.

The children looked at each other in silence. They knew there was nothing more they could do for Peggy now. But what if the medicine *didn't* work? What would they do then?

Back in Oliver West's hut, Ruby gazed out of the window and Oliver and Prince were sitting comfortably by the fire.

"Where can they be?" said Ruby, concerned.

"Don't worry," Oliver reassured her. "Maybe

they stopped over another night."

"No," said Ruby emphatically. "Tomorrow's their wedding day."

"They'll turn up. He's an explorer, isn't he? Knows his way around."

"Huh!" snorted Ruby. "I'm not so sure about that."

"Listen," said Oliver, sensing she was worried, "if they're not here by dawn, we'll go and look for them, right?"

Ruby nodded, relieved that he'd made the suggestion.

"I can just see the headlines: **Famous Explorer Rescued by 'The Maniac'**" said Oliver.

"Maniac?" Ruby looked startled. What had she got herself into?

Oliver smiled. Then he got up and walked over to a newspaper cutting pinned on the wall. It read: **THE MANIAC CRASHES.**

Ruby read out loud: *"Daredevil stunt pilot Oliver West survived a horrifying crash yesterday before a large crowd of people...* You were a stunt pilot?" she asked him.

"'The Maniac'. That's what they called me," he said. "Still, that's all over now. I haven't flown since the crash."

"Why not?" said Ruby.

Oliver held out his hands – they were

trembling. "See that? If I even think about flying, this is what happens."

"I know the feeling," said Ruby, shivering slightly at the memory of her trip into Boluto. Prince barked loudly. "So does he!" she said.

It was clear that nothing would get the three of them up in a plane again.

"Dad?"

It was Peggy! She had moved very slightly where she was lying, covered in foliage that Laura and Mike had piled on top of her to protect her.

"Peggy?" said Laura, waking up from where she'd been dozing beside her sister.

"Peggy!" cried Mike, rushing over to her. "Can you hear me?"

"Well, I'm not deaf!" she grinned at him.

"She's all right," breathed Jack, relief flooding through him.

"Of course I'm all right," said Peggy indignantly, trying to sit up.

"Are you sure?" asked Mike, still worried.

"Yes, I'm sure," she said. "Just feel a bit dizzy, that's all. Is there anything to eat?"

"Typical!" Mike laughed.

Laura turned to Chauca, standing behind them. "Thank you, Chauca!" she said, smiling happily.

Chauca smiled too.

In their cell inside the mountain, Thaddeus and Charlotte tried in vain to think of some way of escaping. And just when they least expected it, the door was flung open by a group of Jaguarheads who dragged the two of them down to the sacrificial area.

Now, firmly bound to stone pillars, Thaddeus and Charlotte could both sense that something was about to happen. Light from the full moon neared the centre of the round window, and steam rose from the well in the middle of the temple.

They looked at Huaman. His face was painted with the weird symbols, and he had been tied inside a cage which was now resting on the rocky floor. As the moon appeared in the centre of the window, the cage was hauled high into the air. The Silverskulls' chanting became more and more frantic and Charlie turned her head away, trying to blot out the terrifying spectacle.

Very slowly, the Silverskulls started to lower the cage again, this time over the well. The steam hissed and curled about it as it moved. By the altar, the High Priestess began to speak, her voice deep and muffled through the horrible mask:

"Oh, Sacred Goddess of the sky, protect us against our enemies and bring evil to those who bring evil to your chosen people! Oh, Sacred

Goddess, hear us! Hear our cries! We cry to you, oh Mighty One!"

The Silverskulls bowed to the goddess. As Huaman was lowered down and down into the jet of steam, his body became a ghost-like figure in the grey vapour. The Silverskulls danced with delight.

Only then did Thaddeus and Charlie realise that the High Priestess had moved nearer to them. Her deep voice echoed through the mask.

"A geological steam vent," she explained, getting pleasure out of their fear.

"It's barbaric!" gasped Charlie.

"I suppose so," intoned the High Priestess, "if you look at it from a certain perspective."

She is clearly quite mad! thought Thaddeus. "Looked at from any perspective!" he shouted at her above the chanting.

"They're totally dominated by the full moon," she went on with her chilling explanation. "Each month, over these two nights, they sacrifice to the moon. If they don't, they believe the moon will die. So, in order to prevent that happening, you will both sink into that vent tomorrow night."

So saying, the High Priestess laughed, the sound echoing above the chanting in a terrifying way.

CHAPTER FIFTEEN

Out on the mountainside, other Silverskulls were moving stealthily through the trees, the moon casting an eerie light on their ghastly forms. They were moving closer and closer to the children's camp, following the orders of their High Priest.

Unaware, the children and Chauca were sitting round their fire.

"Do you know what we're eating?" Jack asked the others.

"What?" said Peggy.

"Maggots," said Jack gleefully.

"Delicious!" Peggy grinned at him. She'd had to get used to a lot of things on this adventure. But right now she was just glad to be alive!

Mike began studying his food uneasily. "Yum, yum," he said grimly.

After a while, the children began to feel better, their spirits restored by the food that Chauca had cooked for them.

Peggy brought out her diary. "Jack, you must tell me what happened when you went off with Chauca," she said, "so I can write it up."

Jack yawned. "Yeah, sometime," he said sleepily. "Not now."

The little group became silent, thinking about their father and Charlie, wondering what the new day would bring. Peggy looked at the flower that Chauca had given her which she'd pressed between the pages of her diary.

"Did you know there's a total eclipse of the moon tomorrow night?" she said idly.

Jack wasn't listening. "I could stay here for ever," he murmured.

"I couldn't," said Laura. "I want to find Dad and Charlotte. Then I just want to go home."

"Me, too," said Mike.

"And then the best thing would be for Dad to stay at home," Laura went on. "Not go away any more."

"I'd like that, too," said Peggy softly.

"Just to have him there all the time..." thought Jack aloud.

"...Never wondering if we'd ever see him again..." said Peggy, yawning.

Above them, the Silverskulls were looking down on their camp, the light of the fire reflected in their horrible eyes.

"...Just a family..." Laura continued.

"Yes, I'd like that. All together." Peggy was nearly asleep now.

"What do you want, Chauca?" asked Jack.

"Drive evil spirits away from my land..." he whispered, looking up at the mountain.

He didn't see the Silverskulls creeping round

the edge of the camp, hidden by the trees. No one saw them.

"Build up my people," he went on. "Be the Tracker tribe again."

"We all want the same thing, really, don't we?" said Peggy.

"A family," said Jack.

They were all feeling sleepy and content round the comfort of the fire when, suddenly, the Silverskulls struck. They whipped out of the darkness like ghastly ghosts, gathered up the children who, taken by surprise, screamed and struggled in vain.

The cockatoo screeched a horrible cry as they were dragged off into the darkness. The Birdwoman, on the edge of the jungle clearing, listened and watched, a silent feathered figure in the darkness.

The Silverskulls dragged the protesting children, and Chauca, up the moonlit mountain track until they reached the rock face with the stone doorway. There, one of them pulled aside the stone which caused the rock to grind open, revealing the dark chasm inside.

The children were bundled inside the mountain, where torches spluttered along the tunnel. They were dazed and confused and felt a sense of mounting fear.

When they came to the fiery pit, they stood close to each other, wondering what was going to happen next. Their guards hustled them towards the flames and, as the tree trunk was held steady, they were shoved across, their hearts in their mouths, terrified of slipping into the pit.

Bruised and shaky, the children were led roughly along the rocky tunnel and into the temple. Here they were pushed unceremoniously into a small prison cell where they fell inside in a heap together on the bare floor. As their eyes got used to the darkness, they began to see what was going on around them, but the sight of what was happening outside the bars of their prison was something they'd rather not have known about.

As the children lay on the prison floor, the cockatoo perched nearby, out of sight. It had flown into the tunnel behind them.

Inside Oliver West's hut, Ruby was asleep on the sofa, a blanket pulled up to her chin, exhausted after her night in the Land Rover. Through her confused dreams of mountains and strange statues, and people being late for weddings, she heard the sound of Prince's barking.

She woke up, rubbing her eyes, not sure where she was. Then she remembered. The sound of Prince's barking outside made her get up.

She threw off the blanket. "Prince?" she called.

Outside the hut, the dog was pulling at an old tarpaulin with his teeth, then dropping it and barking. It was covering something very large but Ruby hadn't got a clue what it could be.

"Prince? What is it?" she said, as she came out of the hut, wondering what on earth Prince was playing at.

He picked up the tarpaulin in his teeth again, tugging violently at the corner. Suddenly, it fell to the ground, revealing a brightly painted helicopter with a face painted on it.

"Oh, my goodness!" breathed Ruby, staring at it.

Woken by the persistent barking, Oliver appeared, running his hands through his tousled hair and standing in the doorway of the hut.

"Is that yours?" Ruby called to him.

"Yeah," he said, nodding.

"Can you fly it?" she said.

"Not any more," he said firmly.

"But you could?" said Ruby. "I mean, if you were looking for someone who was lost in the jungle, say… theoretically speaking, you could fly it?" she added.

"I told you," said Oliver gruffly, "I haven't flown for years, not since the…" He found it difficult even to say the word 'crash'.

Prince barked at both of them, then he hopped up into the open cockpit of the helicopter.

"Oh, no, you don't!" said Ruby.

"They're *your* friends," Oliver said to her.

"You're not getting me in that thing. No way!"

"Good. 'Cos I'm not going to fly it," said Oliver. And they looked at each other and nodded in agreement.

Inside their prison cell, Thaddeus and Charlotte were beginning to feel utterly hopeless.

"Well, today's the day," Thaddeus said, turning to Charlie.

"Yeah," she said softly.

"Tonight… we end up as steamed pudding," he said, grinning ruefully.

"That's not even funny!" gasped Charlie.

"I wasn't trying to be funny," said Thaddeus, his face set in grim lines.

Suddenly, they heard a commotion outside their prison cell, and Thaddeus peered through the bars. "Charlie! Charlie, look!" he called in horror.

CHAPTER SIXTEEN

Reluctantly, Charlie moved to Thaddeus's side and looked through the bars. She saw the children being hustled roughly out of their cell by the Jaguarheads.

"Charlie, they've got the children!" said Thaddeus, gripping the bars.

"Where are they taking them?" she cried as the children were marched down the stairs past their cell.

"Presumably to visit our mad jailer," said Thaddeus cynically.

The children disappeared into the temple, the Jaguarheads shoving them brutally as they went.

"Let me go!" screamed Peggy.

Thaddeus turned white when he heard his daughter's voice. "I'm such a fool!" he choked, turning to Charlie. "A stupid fool! Why didn't I keep my mouth shut?"

"Stop blaming yourself!" said Charlie, putting her hand on Thaddeus's shoulder.

"I've got to get out of here," Thaddeus said hoarsely. "I've got to save the children!"

The helicopter stood on the ground outside Oliver's hut, a silent reminder to Oliver that he should perhaps be doing something to help those people who might be lost or in trouble somewhere in the jungle.

Ruby stood with Prince by the Land Rover, watching Oliver as he paced round his helicopter, checking it over for flying. Her own fear of flying was worse than Oliver's.

"No, Prince. It was bad enough in an aeroplane. But a helicopter... no. I'm not going up in that thing!"

Prince barked, looking up at her.

"No, I'm not," she repeated. "Just stop nagging me!"

Prince barked again.

"Read my lips," said Ruby under her breath. "*I-am-not-going-in-a-helicopter.* Got it?"

Prince barked again. Then, turning once more to look back at Ruby, he headed for the helicopter.

The circle of light from the full moon shone in the centre of the temple where the Silverskulls' chanting still continued rhythmically. The children were dragged into the sacred area by the Jaguarheads and tied up to the pillars. Laura, curious as well as frightened, tried to sneak a glance at the High Priestess in her ominous mask.

"What is this place?" Jack whispered.

"Looks like a temple," said Peggy.

Quite suddenly, as if by magic, the white cockatoo appeared from nowhere, and landed on Laura's shoulder.

"It's Snowy!" she gasped. "Where are we, Snowy? Where are we?"

"What's going to happen to us?" Jack asked the others.

"Skulls!" growled Chauca through clenched teeth.

"What do they want with us?" asked Mike.

"Chauca?" Peggy turned to him for an explanation, her eyes fearful.

"Bad men!" he said fiercely.

"Yes, we know that part." Jack was cynical.

Laura had turned very white. "I feel funny," she said faintly.

"Well, I'm not laughing. We've got to get out of here."

"What can we do?" said Mike in despair.

Peggy turned to Laura at her side. She was staring fixedly at the goddess, who was standing by a second altar. Suddenly, Snowy took off from Laura's shoulder and flew straight past the goddess. At the same time, a Jaguarhead untied Laura and, taking her arm, led her away, unresisting.

It seemed to the others as if Laura was hypnotised, or in some kind of trance. She moved past the Silverskulls towards the goddess in a daze, the Jaguarhead leading her by the arm, all the time being watched by the High Priestess.

"Well, it would seem that the new goddess has elected herself," she intoned.

The goddess stood up. Laura walked up to her and embraced her. The High Priestess turned towards the other children, who were staring at their sister, horrified.

"Calm yourselves, children," she told them. "Put them in the temple!" she ordered the Jaguarheads. "We'll decide what to do with them later."

The children and Chauca were untied and led away, straining to see what was happening to Laura as they left.

Laura had removed the mask from the goddess and they were gazing intently at each other.

Chauca was looking over his shoulder. "Ayala!" he suddenly shouted.

The High Priestess glided down from her place by the altar, and walked to the top of the steps towards Laura and the goddess. There, she took the sacred mask from a Jaguarhead and placed it over Laura's face. Then she put a long, flowing robe over Laura's head and stood back to look at her.

Laura still did not speak or show any feeling. Escorted by the Jaguarheads and the High Priest, she was led down the steps into the temple and past the ceremonial well. There they guided her towards a stone seat where the Silverskulls gathered round her. The other goddess was led over to the temple area where the rest of the children were.

To Thaddeus and Charlotte watching through the bars of their cell, it was a nightmare. They looked on, horrified, as the Silverskulls bowed repeatedly in front of Laura, their chanting rising and falling in an hypnotic rhythm, the High Priestess beside them.

"What are they doing with Laura?" whispered Charlie desperately.

"Treating her as if she were…"

"…sacred," finished Charlie. "We've got to think of a plan!" She couldn't just stand there watching any longer. They must think of something, some way of getting out of there.

"Plan?" said Thaddeus, his voice choking with emotion. "My only plan is to get my hands on that woman—"

"You can't fight them all, Thaddeus," said Charlie.

"What option to I have? Listen. This is what we'll do."

CHAPTER SEVENTEEN

The children and Chauca gathered round Ayala, the cockatoo now perched on Peggy's shoulder.

"Silverskulls take her. Long ago," Chauca explained. "Made Ayala goddess. But too old now."

"I see. Well, hello, Ayala. My name is Peggy."

"Jack," said Jack.

"Mike." And he leant over to shake her hand. They all smiled at each other.

"I just wish—" said Peggy. She glanced nervously in the direction of the temple, from where she could hear the Silverskulls chanting, bowing down in front of Laura.

"Don't worry, Peggy," said Jack. "They all look a bit fierce – but no one's actually been hurt, have they?"

"Not yet," said Mike. "But they're getting pretty worked up about something down there."

They looked down into the temple below, where the High Priestess had turned towards the round window, looking at the moon.

"The Sacred One has answered us!" her voice echoed. "The Sacred One has given us a new goddess. Tonight she will be crowned in glory. Tonight she will take her place over us. Praise the Sacred One! All praise!"

The Silverskulls' chanting was reaching fever pitch.

The children were confused and afraid. "What are they doing to her?" Jack said to the others.

Ayala whispered something to Chauca.

"Ayala say, Laura new goddess," he said.

"But what does it mean?" asked Mike.

"Sacrifice!" Chauca looked frightened.

"Who are they going to sacrifice?" asked Jack.

The children looked at each other.

"Us?" asked Peggy, her voice shaking. Suddenly, she felt resolved to do something. They couldn't just wait for something to happen to them! "We've got to get out of here!" she whispered fiercely.

"And rescue Laura," said Mike.

"But how do we get past the guards?" Jack was always the practical one.

"There must be a way – otherwise how did the High Priestess get in?"

"You're right. She came in from over there," said Jack, and he pointed to the throne where Ayala was sitting. Carefully, he ran his hands over the panels behind it. Suddenly, the cockatoo flew across and landed on a piece of raised carving next to one of the panels in the back wall of the temple. He pecked at one of the symbols in the centre of the panel.

Jack pushed it, and instantly there was a click as the panel silently slid up and a large opening was revealed. The children were amazed.

Jack pressed the carved symbol again, and the secret door closed with another click. Now for a plan...

Charlotte was standing at the door of their cell, holding on to the bars and shouting.

"Help! Help! Somebody please help me!"

"Keep going, Charlie," urged Thaddeus, who was hiding behind the door.

Charlotte started to groan dramatically as if she was in distress. "Please! Someone help me!"

A Jaguarhead on guard nearby strode over to their cell to investigate. He peered through the bars and saw Charlie writhing on the floor as if in great pain. He grunted, looked around, then opened the cell door. Just as he came in, Thaddeus slammed it hard against the Jaguarhead, who sprawled to the ground, badly winded.

"Come on!" yelled Thaddeus to Charlie.

Quickly they rushed out of the cell, pulling the door shut and bolting it again behind them.

Now outside, they looked around desperately, not knowing which way to go or what to do for the best.

"I'll get that crazy woman!" cried Thaddeus.

"You grab Laura!"

Together, he and Charlie made a dash for it down the steps towards the temple – and Laura. No sooner had they run into the sacred area than Charlie was grabbed by the Silverskulls. Thaddeus, running ahead of her, turned when he heard her shout and went back to try and help.

"Let go of her, you skull-head!" he cried.

But it was no use; Thaddeus knew from the start that they couldn't possibly overcome so many Silverskulls and Jaguarheads.

Up the steps in the temple, the children heard the commotion down below and they crowded together to see what was going on. They could hardly believe their eyes!

"It's Dad!" cried Mike. "And Charlie!"

"Where?" said Peggy, pushing past him to see better.

"Over there!" said Mike, pointing at the throng below.

"They've caught them as well," Jack said despondently.

"Dad doesn't stand a chance against all those skull-heads!" cried Peggy.

"What are they going to do to them?" asked Mike.

"I don't know," said Jack, worried, "but it doesn't look good."

"I don't like this!" Mike looked scared.

"It's OK, Mike." Peggy tried her best to soothe him. "But we've got to think of a way of getting everyone out of here!"

As the children watched, Thaddeus and Charlotte were pushed across the floor of the temple to the foot of the altar. Thaddeus tried to twist round in the grip of the Jaguarheads to see what was happening to Laura, who was sitting motionless on her throne.

"Laura! It's Dad!" he called. "Can you hear me? It's Dad! *Laura*!" He was getting desperate.

But Laura was oblivious of what was going on around her.

As the High Priestess watched, Thaddeus and Charlie were brought to their knees in front of her.

"Don't waste your breath," she snarled. "She belongs to us now."

She motioned to the Jaguarheads to remove Thaddeus and Charlie and they were pulled upright again and dragged painfully across to the columns and tied up. Then the High Priestess, carrying bowls of pigment, came solemnly towards them. She nodded to one of the Jaguarheads, who dipped a finger into the pigment and began to put sacrificial markings on Charlotte's face.

The children watched anxiously from behind the temple seat.

"What are they doing to them?" Mike whispered.

"Ayala say... sacrifice!" said Chauca.

Peggy felt numb. "Sacrifice?" she gasped.

CHAPTER NINETEEN

"Silverskulls sacrifice to keep tribe strong," Chauca said. "When moon is high. When it shine through ring, sacrifice to goddess."

"You mean... to Laura?" blurted out Jack.

"Yes," said Chauca. "Laura goddess now."

"Laura will stop it. She won't let it happen!" said Mike desperately.

"No," said Chauca flatly. "Laura goddess now. She accept sacrifice."

Mike looked across to Laura. She was still sitting motionless on her throne.

"You say – when the moon is high?" asked Peggy.

"Yes," Chauca nodded.

"Can't we *do* anything?" Mike felt so helpless.

"We could get out through the shaft, but then what could we do?" said Jack. "We need a diversion to distract them."

The noise from the Silverskulls was getting louder and louder all the time and the children could sense they didn't have much time left.

"The moon," said Peggy quickly. "It shines through that ring thing over there?" she asked Chauca.

He nodded.

"Looks like the zenith, doesn't it?" she said.

"What happens then?" asked Mike.

"Then they make the sacrifice?" Peggy asked Chauca.

He nodded again.

Peggy had a determined look on her face. "Remember what I said? There's a total eclipse of the moon tonight."

"Ee-clip? What is ee-clip?" Chauca was baffled by the word.

"Eclipse," Peggy explained. "It's when the earth comes between the sun and the moon. The earth's shadow blocks the light from the moon. But what if these people don't know that the moon's going to be eclipsed? What if they don't know about eclipses at all?"

As one, they turned and looked at the moon shining through the round window. Then they looked down at Thaddeus and Charlie again. Their faces were now covered in painted symbols, and they were strapped to the altar.

Thaddeus was still looking at Laura intently. "She hasn't moved for hours," he whispered.

"Maybe they've hypnotised her?" said Charlie.

"She's certainly in some kind of trance," admitted Thaddeus.

"Do you think we'll be all right, then?" Charlie asked him.

"Not looking too good, is it?" he said.

"I love you," said Charlie suddenly.

"I love you, too," said Thaddeus, trying to smile.

"I can't believe it's got to end here."

Charlie's face was breaking his heart. "I can't even kiss you," he said.

"You could close your eyes and pretend," she whispered.

In the temple, the children stood in a knot together.

"Now you all know what you have to do?" whispered Jack.

"Yes," said Peggy. "When you three go down the secret tunnel, Ayala and I will start a diversion."

"But not until the moon reaches the zenith," affirmed Jack.

"But we don't know where the tunnel leads," Mike groaned.

"We can't get out any other way, Mike," Jack told him.

Mike looked at his watch. "Not long to go now," he said, looking down into the temple.

The High Priestess, escorted by Jaguarheads, walked solemnly towards the altar. "The time has come!" she called.

A stir in the middle of the floor made the children look away from the High Priestess, but the sight they saw made them even more frightened.

Thaddeus and Charlotte were being hurried towards the sacred cage by the Jaguarheads. Almost as soon as they were pushed inside, the cage began to rise upwards, until it was suspended high in the air over the well, the steam hissing out from the vent and shrouding them both.

The Silverskulls formed a circle round the cage, chanting and dancing, as the children watched, powerless to help.

Thaddeus and Charlotte, suspended in the cage, clung to each other. Thaddeus turned to look at Laura, pleading with her.

"Laura! Laura!" He tried to shout above the relentless chanting of the Silverskulls.

But Laura still sat, unmoving, framed by the circle of flaming torches, looking beautiful, distant and implacable behind her mask.

"It's no good, Thad!" cried Charlie.

Below them, the High Priestess began the ritual.

"The time comes!" she wailed.

The moon cast its beam spookily on to the middle of the floor. "The time of the new goddess!" she intoned.

Thaddeus and Charlie looked at each other helplessly.

In the temple, Peggy turned to Ayala, nervous but determined. "We'd better get started," she said. And they disappeared behind the altar.

The cage swung higher, carrying its sacrificial victims to the rocky ceiling and the Silverskulls danced round it, swaying and chanting.

Behind the altar, Ayala placed her robe over Peggy's head, and at the back of the temple, Mike, Jack and Chauca stood by the secret entrance. Jack pressed the carved symbol and the panel slid open. He peered inside nervously. Suddenly, the white cockatoo flew past him into the mouth of the entrance.

"Jack!" called Peggy. "It's a sign. The bird's showing the way to go!"

Jack slipped through the opened panel doorway and started down a ladder suspended immediately inside. Without warning, he stopped.

"Go on, Jack!" said Mike.

"But there might be more Silverskulls!" said Jack, frightened of the unknown.

Behind the altar, Ayala held the mask ready to place on Peggy's head, on top of the robe.

"I hope this is going to work, Ayala. Ready?" Ayala nodded.

Peggy felt very nervous as she felt the mask

going over her head and covering her face. "Please let them believe I'm a goddess!" she whispered to herself.

Ahead of the boys, the cockatoo fluttered backwards and forwards in the tunnel, trying to tell them something. Cautiously, Jack, Mike and Chauca went down the stone steps.

"Which way?" said Mike.

Jack shrugged. He hadn't got a clue, he'd lost all sense of direction inside the mountain. "This way!" he said suddenly, pointing at the bird. "He's guiding us!"

CHAPTER TWENTY

The boys turned down the tunnel, following the white cockatoo flying ahead of them until they reached the end. Cautiously they crept out into the temple, near the pillars. Jack glanced towards the round window carved out of the rock face. "I hope the eclipse is on time!" he said.

"The diary couldn't be wrong, could it?" asked Mike.

"It had better not be!" Jack whispered.

They moved silently along the wall, hidden in the shadows behind the pillars, the people on the floor distracted by the ceremony.

The boys looked once more at the window. "What's keeping it?" asked Jack desperately.

The moon slid slowly towards the centre of the opening, casting its beams on the rocky floor, and creeping towards the new goddess – Laura.

As the moon started to fill the window, the High Priestess cast herself full-length on the floor in front of Laura, and the Silverskulls did the same. A shaft of moonlight crept slowly towards Laura as the cage, suspended above, creaked closer and closer to the well.

Suddenly, a high-pitched wailing began from the temple and everyone turned to see what was happening. Peggy, dressed as Ayala, came to the edge of the temple steps and started to walk down them. Ayala kept on chanting and when Peggy reached the foot of the steps, she walked purposefully across the temple towards the round window.

The High Priestess gestured to the Jaguarheads. "Stop her!" she screamed. "Stop her!"

The Silverskulls and Jaguarheads watched, transfixed, but nobody moved. Framed in the hoop of the round rocky window, Peggy raised her arms to the moon as it finally filled the space, then turned and called out, not knowing whether she would be understood or not.

"The goddess eats the moon!"

Just in time, a tiny piece of moon began to disappear, as if it had been bitten from the rim. The Silverskulls dropped to their knees in front of Peggy, stunned, and Thaddeus and Charlotte stared at her in amazement.

Ayala kept up her wailing in a high-pitched tone. The boys headed towards the well, seized the ropes and pulleys which tethered the cage, and began to lower it to the ground.

Peggy stayed in front of the round window, her arms raised. "The goddess eats the moon!" she repeated in a voice she hoped would be convincing.

As more and more of the moon began to disappear, the Silverskulls and Jaguarheads lay prone on the floor, too frightened to move, convinced that the end of the world was about to happen.

"Stop her!" yelled the High Priestess. Now she'd got over her surprise at Peggy's appearance, she wasn't fooled for one moment.

But no one listened to her, they were too preoccupied with the moon, rapidly disappearing in front of their eyes.

The boys worked quickly, releasing Thaddeus and Charlotte from the cage.

"Good lads!" gasped Thaddeus. "Good lads! You get the girls and head for the tunnel. We'll get Laura!"

As the boys ran towards Peggy, Chauca gestured to Ayala to come with them. Thaddeus and Charlotte moved swiftly across to Laura as the eclipse continued.

"Laura, it's me, Dad!" said Thaddeus, shaking her slightly. "Stop it now! We've got to get out of here!"

Laura seemed to shift restlessly and shook her head from side to side. "No! No!" she wailed. "I want to stay! I want to stay!"

"Laura, please!" begged Thaddeus. "Time's running out, we've got to go!"

Laura took a deep breath, "I have to stay!" she wailed again.

The High Priestess had come up behind Thaddeus and Charlotte and Laura ran straight past them and into the High Priestess's arms, turning to look defiantly at her father, like a stranger.

"She's mine!" said the High Priestess triumphantly.

"Laura!" pleaded Thaddeus. Then he turned to the High Priestess. "Let her go!" he shouted.

"What? So that you can destroy years of my work?" she said, her voice hard and cruel. She moved with Laura towards the well.

"No!" cried Thaddeus. "Give her back and I promise I won't say a word about this to a living soul. None of us will."

"No!" said the High Priestess. "I want to keep *her*!"

"Let her go!" said Thaddeus again. "Please! I'll take her place, if you like. I'll stay. I'll be your hostage!"

But the High Priestess was unmoved. "I want to keep *her*!" she cried.

Charlotte crept unnoticed behind the High Priestess, who was caught up in her argument with Thaddeus. She raised her clenched fists above her head and hit the High Priestess with all her might on the back of the neck, knocking her over.

Instantly, Thaddeus grabbed Laura, lifting her off her feet and following Charlotte as she led the way out.

The High Priestess sprawled on the ground, her hideous mask knocked off her head. Suddenly, she looked pathetic and powerless.

Jack, Mike and Peggy, with Chauca and Ayala, were waiting at the mouth of the tunnel as Charlotte and Thaddeus, carrying the struggling Laura, ran towards them. Swiftly, a Jaguarhead stepped in front of them, but Charlotte, her energy returned, knocked her aside with one blow.

"Nice one, Charlie!" called Thaddeus proudly, and they hurried on towards the children.

"Keep moving!" he called to them as they came near. "Keep moving! There's no time to waste!" He turned in the tunnel to see if anyone was following them. Ahead, the way was lit with torches.

Thaddeus turned to Chauca. "Chauca! Grab a torch!" he called. "Hurry! Hurry!"

And they sped on again, Chauca running ahead, holding the flaming torch aloft.

Inside the temple, the moon began to reappear

from the shadow of the earth once more. Aware that the sacred light was coming back, the Silverskulls and Jaguarheads slowly raised their heads with cries of relief.

The High Priestess, on her feet again, ran among them, ranting and raving. But she had forgotten to put on her mask. The Silverskulls stood up slowly, staring at her.

"Get them!" the High Priestess was screaming at the Silverskulls. "Go on! Get them! Don't just stand there staring!"

Suddenly, her hand came up to her face. She realised she had forgotten to put on her mask! As she stood there, revealed as a small, mousy-looking woman, the Silverskulls moved menacingly towards her. She started to back away towards the well.

"Stop!" she yelled. "Stop! I can explain!"

But the Silverskulls took no notice as they moved relentlessly nearer and nearer.

CHAPTER TWENTY-ONE

In the tunnel, the torchlight flickered on the rocky walls as the children and Thaddeus and Charlotte made their way, stumbling and breathing hard, back towards the cave entrance and the fiery pit, spanned by the rolling log. As they approached, they saw the cockatoo perched on the other side, waiting for them.

"There's the bird!" shouted Mike.

"We've no time for birdwatching, Mike," said Thaddeus. "Keep going!"

"Thaddeus!" called Charlie. "It's dangerous!"

Thaddeus stood on the edge of the pit, panting from carrying Laura and running down the tunnel. "Wait! Wait! Wait!" he called to the others. "We need to think this through. Mike, you and Peggy take... take this girl," he said, nodding in Ayala's direction.

"Ayala," said Peggy.

"You three go across first," Thaddeus went on. "Charlie, you're next with Laura. Chauca. Jack, then you. Jack, lend me a hand here first. You'll have to hold the far end when I come across."

Thaddeus and Jack knelt down and braced themselves on the end of the log. "OK," called Thaddeus. "Off you go!"

Mike started across the trunk, wobbling slightly and trying not to look down at the flames beneath him. When he reached the other side, Peggy began to cross, then Ayala.

When they'd crossed over, they braced themselves on the far end of the log, then Laura was helped across by Charlotte. But halfway across Laura suddenly pushed forward, away from Charlotte, wobbling and flailing her arms, and nearly sending them both into the chasm. Frantically, Charlie managed to regain her balance.

"Laura!" she called out, trying to keep her voice calm. "Keep moving!"

"Laura!" yelled Thaddeus from behind them. "Stop it!"

Stumbling and frightened, Charlotte and Laura reached the other side of the pit, and Thaddeus turned to Chauca, nodding for him to start across, knowing that at any moment the Silverskulls would have seen the moonlight reappear, and give chase to them.

Now, Jack made his way carefully across the log.

"Jack, Chauca," called Thaddeus. "Hold the other end!"

The children all held the end of the log as Thaddeus started to cross. "Here I come!" he called.

He picked up the torch and stepped onto the trunk – but the children couldn't hold it against Thaddeus's weight! It began to spin wildly as Thaddeus stepped on to it. His arms flailed as he tried to keep his balance, then he managed to jump off again.

"Peggy!" called Charlie on the other side. "Hang on to Laura!" and she started to help Jack and Chauca stop the log from spinning.

"Hold on!" she called encouragingly.

Peggy grabbed her sister, who began to struggle violently. "Someone help me!" she cried. "I can't hold her!"

Thaddeus stepped gingerly onto the log once more, but his heavier weight made the log begin to spin again. The rest of them on the other side used every ounce of their strength to hold it still.

Thaddeus was halfway across when their strength began to fail and the log slipped round, almost a full turn. The fiery torch flew out of Thaddeus's hand into the chasm below.

"I can't hold it!" cried Jack, lying with all his weight on the end of the log.

"Nor me!" shouted Chauca.

"Thaddeus!" screamed Charlotte.

Thaddeus's feet had slipped and his arms shot into the air as he fell. Somehow, he managed to fling his arms round the log and hang on while the others strained to hold the trunk steady.

Gradually, he hauled himself grimly back up onto the log. Then, balancing precariously, and getting to his feet unsteadily, he made a mad dash for the safety of the other side.

"Phew!" he gasped, as he stepped on to the cave floor. "That was close! Thanks. Come on, guys!"

They all turned and started down the tunnel again, with Laura still struggling and moaning.

"Come *on*!" Charlie said to her desperately, knowing that at any moment the Silverskulls would be upon them.

The faithful bird flew ahead of them down the dark tunnel to the rock door where they had first entered the cave.

"How do we get out?" Jack called back to the others.

"There must be a way. Look for a lever or something," said Thaddeus.

Jack fumbled with his fingers on the rock face, scratching his knuckles. "I can't see anything!" he called desperately.

"Nor can I, Thaddeus," said Charlie.

Jack suddenly shouted. "The cockatoo!"

"Yes!" said Mike.

"It showed us the way out of the temple! Maybe it can do the same here!" said Jack excitedly.

"Show us the way out! Please!" Peggy begged the bird.

The cockatoo flew along the rocky face of the tunnel wall, his wing tips scraping its surface. He landed to one side and the others peered into the darkness. They could just make out a row of carved square pegs on a ledge, with symbols on them. Thaddeus walked over to them.

"Which one do we pull?" asked Mike.

"Um… eeny, meeny, miny, mo…" muttered Thaddeus.

He pulled one at random and a low rumble could be heard behind them.

"Dad!" shrieked Peggy.

Thaddeus turned round. A different opening in another part of the tunnel had appeared. Chauca let out a strangled cry. He ran to the opening and disappeared through it.

"Chauca!" called Peggy. "Come back!" And she ran after him.

"Peggy! Chauca! Come back!" shouted Thaddeus. "You're going the wrong way! Come back! You're heading deeper into the mountain!"

Peggy hesitated for an instant, but went on after Chauca.

"Peggy!" called Thaddeus again.

But Peggy was determined to follow Chauca.

He was running, bent double, through what looked like an old mining tunnel. Suddenly, ahead of them, Chauca and Peggy saw men working with pick axes and shovels, looking thin and cowed. This was the mine!

A sudden shout in front of her brought Peggy to her senses.

"Huaman!" It was Chauca – he had seen his uncle.

Huaman turned, unbelieving, "*Masuri!*" he shouted back.

But a rasping sound behind them made Chauca and Peggy turn round fearfully. The door in the tunnel had closed behind them.

CHAPTER TWENTY-TWO

Thaddeus was pulling each of the carved symbols in turn, desperate to open the door out of the cave.

"Come *on*, Thaddeus!" urged Charlotte.

"I *am* coming on, Charlie. But nothing's happening!" he said.

"Maybe it's a combination, Dad?" Jack suggested.

"Yes," said Charlotte, "like a combination puzzle!"

"Well, you have a go, Jack," said Thaddeus, moving aside for his adopted son. "I was never any good at combination puzzles."

Peggy was standing beside the door when it opened once more. Chauca motioned to his fellow Trackers to follow him. "*Ansuli!*" he called. "*Koomba!*"

Carrying their tools, Huaman and the other Trackers followed Chauca and Peggy out of the mine that had been their prison for so long, and down the tunnel towards the rock door. Jack and Thaddeus were still desperately trying to open it.

Not far behind Thaddeus and the children, the Silverskulls had reached the fiery pit and were holding the log while the first of their group ran across it. They were determined to catch the enemies who had snatched their sacrifice.

Outside Oliver West's hut, Ruby clutched on to Prince as the helicopter prepared for take-off. As the rotor blades gathered speed, Oliver looked across at her. They gripped hands for a moment, then Oliver guided the helicopter slowly up into the air.

"We're going up!" squealed Ruby. "We're going up! Oh… Prince!" She clung on to Prince for dear life. "Don't look down," she said to him. "Whatever you do, Prince, don't look down!"

And she covered Prince's eyes with her hands, and shut her own eyes as well. Moments later, in spite of herself, she peeked down, just for a second. She saw that the helicopter was above a forest. It was too much for Ruby.

"I must be mad!" she moaned, shutting her eyes again quickly.

Jack was wildly trying every combination he could think of, the others watching him anxiously. Precious seconds were ticking away. All of them could sense that the Silverskulls were closing in on them.

"Quick, Jack!" begged Charlotte.

"It's no good!" he said. "I've tried everything!"

Then, as if out of nowhere, Peggy, Chauca, Huaman and all the other Trackers arrived in the tunnel behind them.

"Huaman!" cried Charlotte.

"My people!" said Chauca, tears in his eyes.

"Trackers?" asked Thaddeus, not quite believing what he saw.

"Not dead," said Chauca, nodding.

"They weren't actually sacrificed at all," said Peggy, coming up to her father. "They were making them work down the mine."

"Well, that's great they're alive," said Thaddeus, grinning. "But we still have to get out of here!"

Jack was still trying desperately to find the right combinations when the cockatoo flew onto Ayala's shoulder and gave a piercing cry.

"What's it doing?" asked Charlotte. Jack pulled two levers together and then stood back, amazed. There was a grinding sound and a rumble of rocks as the entrance moved slowly aside, and the cockatoo flew out.

"Everybody out!" shouted Thaddeus. "Move it!"

"*Oomba!*" shouted Chauca to the other Trackers.

Thaddeus stood to one side to let them through, then he lifted Laura, still dazed, and carried her outside.

Mike hung back inside the entrance. "How does it work?" he mumbled, shaking his head.

"Come on, Mike!" ordered Thaddeus. "Before it's too late!"

Mike, always fascinated with mechanical things, couldn't resist giving the levers one more pull to see if he could figure out the combination.

Thaddeus turned round from where he had joined the others outside. "Mike!" he yelled. "Leave it!"

An ominous rumble started in the tunnel, and the rocky entrance was starting to close.

Mike darted to the opening. "Dad!" he cried out.

"Mike!" yelled Thaddeus.

The door was closing fast, grinding and rumbling as it slid over the rocky floor. Thaddeus ran to the opening and grabbed Mike's arm just as the gap had narrowed to a slit. He pulled Mike violently through the entrance in the nick of time and the rock door thudded shut behind him.

Inside, the first Silverskull had reached the entrance and grabbed at the lever to keep it open. Mike fell on to the grass outside, recovering from his close shave, and then the rock door ground open again.

"They're coming!" yelled Thaddeus.

He grabbed a pick axe from one of the Trackers, and swung it into the stone squares at the side of the entrance. The rock stopped moving, leaving only a small gap. Howls of rage could be heard inside as the upper body of a Silverskull groped through the gap in a useless attempt to get out. Other Silverskulls behind him were pushing him and trying to force the rock door open again.

Thaddeus didn't want to hang about any longer. He lifted Laura up and started down the mountain with Charlotte and the others following.

"Let's put some distance behind us!" he called urgently.

Huaman had led his group into a clearing. For the first time, the Trackers could enjoy being free again. Thaddeus put Laura down carefully on the ground so that he could say goodbye to the Trackers. Charlotte and the children smiled at their new friends.

Chauca spoke to his tribe, telling them to run, to go back home. "My family. Trackers," he said proudly to Thaddeus. "*Omna*! Trackers! *Omna*!" he said to them, waving at them to leave quickly.

Smiling and nodding, they started to run down the mountainside, back to the home they had been taken from.

Thaddeus knelt down in front of Laura. She was murmuring something, as though she had a fever.

"Pl... please! Go... go back! Let me go back...! I want to go back! Let me go back!" she kept saying.

The others looked at her anxiously. "Can't we help her?" said Jack.

"I wish I knew how," whispered Thaddeus, his face grim, and Laura went suddenly limp in his arms.

"Laura! Laura!" cried Thaddeus urgently.

In the helicopter, Ruby was gaining confidence. She was even looking at the ground beneath her.

"If they've lit a fire," she said, a worried look on her face, "we'd be able to see it, right?"

Prince barked.

"Oh, you think they have, Prince?" she said.

The dog barked again.

"Yeah," said Ruby ruefully. "You're such an optimist, Prince."

She turned her head to peer down at the forest again. It looked so dense she couldn't imagine ever being able to find the family, and there certainly didn't seem to be any sign of them. Where could they be?

CHAPTER TWENTY-THREE

In the clearing everyone gathered round Laura.

"Thaddeus," said Charlotte, "we've got to move on! The Silverskulls and those others will catch up with us soon!" There was a note of desperation in her voice.

"Look!" cried Mike suddenly, pointing.

On the edge of the clearing, almost invisible in the trees, stood the Birdwoman.

"What on earth...?!" gasped Charlotte.

"What's she doing?" whispered Peggy.

The Birdwoman came nearer.

"Who is she?" asked Charlotte quietly. She had never seen such a strange creature. Her hair was a mass of feathers, falling down her arms to her feathery fingers.

"She guided us through the tunnels," whispered Jack.

The Birdwoman raised her arms. Her voice was deep and echoing in Laura's head. "Come back, my child," she called. "Come back!"

Laura stirred in her father's arms and opened her eyes. "Dad?" she said in a normal voice.

"Laura?" A look of huge relief spread over Thaddeus's face.

"Dad!" said Laura. "You're safe! You're back!"

"And so are you, my love," whispered

Thaddeus as he hugged her.

Not far behind them, the rock face opened once more, and the Silverskulls surged through, making their way through the trees to the family group.

Thaddeus heard a noise behind him in the forest and turned his head, listening.

"What is it?" asked Charlotte.

As she spoke, the Silverskulls had formed a circle around them as they emerged from the forest.

"Dad!" shrieked Peggy.

"Don't move!" he ordered them. "Don't move! Easy…"

As if out of nowhere, they suddenly heard the roar of the helicopter. It surged over the tree tops, its blades whirring noisily. The Silverskulls, terrified by the huge, strange machine, scattered in all directions, vanishing into the forest on either side.

Above them, the helicopter hovered for a moment, then started to descend. The children jumped up and down in excitement, calling out and waving their arms around.

"It's Ruby!" yelled Mike. "It's Ruby!"

"They've gone!" shouted Peggy, turning round to look for the Silverskulls. "The helicopter scared them away!"

"Just in the nick of time," breathed Charlotte.

Ruby jumped down from the helicopter and ran towards the children. As they fell on her, she hugged them all tightly. There was a bark from the helicopter.

"Prince!" shouted Laura.

"Well," said Ruby, "I've never had that effect on anyone before. Hey, what's with the warpaint?" she asked.

"Oh," said Thaddeus, shaking his head wearily and smiling at her, "it's a long story. I have to say that was quite an entrance, Ruby."

"I thought you didn't like flying?" said Jack.

"Oh," said Ruby, nonchalantly, "nothing to it." And she laughed.

"Chauca," said Charlotte, "we haven't had a chance to meet your friend properly, yet."

"This is Ayala," said Chauca, smiling. "She from my tribe."

"The High Priestess was wicked to chain all your people up and make them work like that," said Peggy.

"Greed corrupts, Peggy," Thaddeus said, putting his hand on her shoulder.

"And she was no High Priestess," said Charlotte. "I'm so glad your people were saved, Huaman."

"Thank you from all our people," said

Huaman gravely. Then he turned to Chauca and Ayala. "Come," he said, and he turned and left them.

"We go now," said Chauca, looking at them all. "Ayala and Chauca. Together." Chauca took her hand.

"Thank you for all you've done for us. Goodbye," said Thaddeus.

"'Bye," they all called. "Goodbye."

"Good luck," whispered Peggy.

And Chauca and Ayala turned and disappeared into the forest.

"Well, looks like there's two weddings happening around here," Ruby grinned.

"You should have been there, Ruby. I thought we'd never get out," said Peggy dramatically.

"Well, we did," said Thaddeus, standing with his arm round Charlotte. "Thanks to you lot."

"You were all very brave," Charlie said.

"I'm very proud of you. And there's something I want to say. While Charlie and I were in that cage, waiting to be... what's the word?" said Thaddeus.

"Barbecued?" offered Peggy.

"More like steamed!" said Mike.

"Right!" Thaddeus grinned. "Steamed. I was thinking... I haven't seen enough of you lot. I spend my time wandering off around the world, missing out on the good times. Well, all that's going to change. From now on I'm staying at home, with you and Charlie."

"And Ruby, and Prince!" cried the children.

"And Ruby and Prince," Thaddeus agreed.

"Yeah!" they shouted.

"Dad?" said Laura quietly.

"Yes, Laura?" said Thaddeus.

"That woman. That bird," she said, puzzled.

"The light can play strange tricks in the jungle, Laura. Some things can't easily be explained."

Thaddeus put his other arm round Laura, and together they walked towards the helicopter.

CHAPTER TWENTY-FOUR

A DC3 aircraft flew noisily through the sky.

On board, a vicar declared: "I now pronounce you man and wife…"

A wedding ring was produced and placed on the bride's finger. Charlotte flexed the finger nervously and glanced at Thaddeus. The two of them were standing in front of the vicar, who was holding a bible.

"You may kiss the bride," he said to Thaddeus.

Thaddeus and Charlotte kissed each other and turned to the children, and Ruby, who stood smiling at them, all dressed in their smart wedding gear.

Unusually for a bridal couple, Thaddeus and Charlotte were wearing parachutes as well. Now they walked together to the side of the plane.

Charlotte handed her bouquet to Ruby. "'Bye, darlings," she said. "We'll see you soon."

"Be good, now," said Thaddeus. "Do as Ruby tells you."

"'Bye!" said the children, exchanging grins.

Thaddeus and Charlotte stepped out into thin air and the children and Ruby waved as the happy couple went into free-fall for a few metres before their chutes snapped open. Prince barked excitedly.

＊

Down on the island, Charlotte and Thaddeus landed on the firm white sand of a beautiful beach, their parachutes collapsing with a sigh around them. They quickly slipped off their harnesses and hugged each other.

"Alone at last!" said Thaddeus, grinning at his new bride.

They were just moving closer together, happiness shining in their eyes, when there was a shout from above.

"Look out! No brakes!" It was Mike!

Thaddeus and Charlotte looked up at the sky. It was not just Mike, it was *all* the children, parachuting down to the beach. First Mike landed, then Peggy.

"Yeah! Here I come!" yelled Jack as he landed.

Then came Laura. Soon all the children, grinning from ear to ear, thumped down beside Thaddeus and Charlotte, who were standing speechless on the beach. Above them, they heard something else that sounded very much like a dog barking! Everyone except Laura looked amazed as Prince parachuted into view, looking perfectly happy but a bit windblown.

"Well," said Laura, "I couldn't leave Prince behind, could I?"

Everyone burst out laughing.

"Hey, look!" shouted Thaddeus.

The aeroplane was making a low pass over the sea in front of them. There was Ruby, giving them a thumbs-up sign from the window. They all had a feeling that this was going to be the best honeymoon ever!

Order Form

To order direct from the publishers, just make a list of the titles you want and fill in the form below:

Name

....

Address

....

....

....

Send to: Dept 6, HarperCollins Publishers Ltd, Westerhill Road, Bishopbriggs, Glasgow G64 2QT.

Please enclose a cheque or postal order to the value of the cover price, plus:

UK & BFPO: Add £1.00 for the first book, and 25p per copy for each additional book ordered.

Overseas and Eire: Add £2.95 service charge. Books will be sent by surface mail but quotes for airmail despatch will be given on request.

A 24-hour telephone ordering service is available to holders of Visa, MasterCard, Amex or Switch cards on 0141-772 2281.

Collins
An *Imprint* of HarperCollins*Publishers*